James Hadley Chase and The Murder Room

〉〉〉 This title is part of The Murder Room, our series dedicated to making available out-of-print or hard-to-find titles by classic crime writers.

Crime fiction has always held up a mirror to society. The Victorians were fascinated by sensational murder and the emerging science of detection; now we are obsessed with the forensic detail of violent death. And no other genre has so captivated and enthralled readers.

Vast troves of classic crime writing have for a long time been unavailable to all but the most dedicated frequenters of second-hand bookshops. The advent of digital publishing means that we are now able to bring you the backlists of a huge range of titles by classic and contemporary crime writers, some of which have been out of print for decades.

From the genteel amateur private eyes of the Golden Age and the femmes fatales of pulp fiction, to the morally ambiguous hard-boiled detectives of mid twentieth-century America and their descendants who walk our twenty-first century streets, The Murder Room has it all. 〉〉〉

The Murder Room
Where Criminal Minds

themurderroom.com

T0352487

James Hadley Chase (1906–1985)

Born René Brabazon Raymond in London, the son of a British colonel in the Indian Army, James Hadley Chase was educated at King's School in Rochester, Kent, and left home at the age of 18. He initially worked in book sales until, inspired by the rise of gangster culture during the Depression and by reading James M. Cain's *The Postman Always Rings Twice*, he wrote his first novel, *No Orchids for Miss Blandish*. Despite the American setting of many of his novels, Chase (like Peter Cheyney, another hugely successful British noir writer) never lived there, writing with the aid of maps and a slang dictionary. He had phenomenal success with the novel, which continued unabated throughout his entire career, spanning 45 years and nearly 90 novels. His work was published in dozens of languages and over thirty titles were adapted for film. He served in the RAF during World War II, where he also edited the RAF Journal. In 1956 he moved to France with his wife and son; they later moved to Switzerland, where Chase lived until his death in 1985.

By James Hadley Chase
(published in The Murder Room)

No Orchids for Miss Blandish
Eve
More Deadly Than the Male
Mission to Venice
Mission to Siena
Not Safe to Be Free
Shock Treatment
Come Easy – Go Easy
What's Better Than Money?
Just Another Sucker
I Would Rather Stay Poor
A Coffin from Hong Kong
Tell it to the Birds
One Bright Summer Morning
The Soft Centre
You Have Yourself a Deal
Have This One on Me
Well Now, My Pretty
Believed Violent
An Ear to the Ground
The Whiff of Money
The Vulture Is a Patient Bird
Like a Hole in the Head
An Ace Up My Sleeve

Want to Stay Alive?
Just a Matter of Time
You're Dead Without Money
Have a Change of Scene
Knock, Knock! Who's There?
Goldfish Have No Hiding Place
So What Happens to Me?
The Joker in the Pack
Believe This, You'll Believe
  Anything
Do Me a Favour – Drop Dead
I Hold the Four Aces
My Laugh Comes Last
Consider Yourself Dead
You Must Be Kidding
A Can of Worms
Try This One for Size
You Can Say That Again
Hand Me a Fig-Leaf
Have a Nice Night
We'll Share a Double Funeral
Not My Thing
Hit Them Where It Hurts

Goldfish Have No Hiding Place

James Hadley Chase

An Orion book

Copyright © Hervey Raymond 1974

The right of James Hadley Chase to be identified as the author of this work has been asserted in accordance with the Copyright, Designs and Patents Act 1988.

This edition published by
The Orion Publishing Group Ltd
Orion House
5 Upper St Martin's Lane
London WC2H 9EA

An Hachette UK company
A CIP catalogue record for this book is available from the British Library

ISBN 978 1 4719 0384 7

www.orionbooks.co.uk

ON THIS hot Sunday afternoon, as I had the house to myself, I decided it would be an opportunity to take a close look at myself, to consider if there was anything I could do to bridge the widening gap between Linda and myself, and to examine my financial position which was far from healthy.

Linda was with the Mitchells. I had begged off, explaining I had work to do. Linda had shrugged, taken her swim suit and had driven over to the Mitchell's house with my vague promise I would join them later. I knew she wouldn't care if I showed up or not.

Because of a defective filter in my pool, this was one of the very rare Sundays when I could be on my own: an opportunity I wasn't going to miss.

So I sat in the sun and looked at myself. I am thirty-eight years of age, physically fit and blessed with a creative brain. Some three years ago, I had been a successful columnist for the *Los Angeles Herald*. The work had bored me, but it was a way to earn a decent living, and as I had just married Linda who had extravagant tastes, earning a decent living was important.

One evening, in San Francisco, I attended one of those dreary cocktail parties where the Big-wheels meet and talk business while their wives yak in the background. There was little in it for me, but if I hadn't shown up I might have missed something and I made a point of never missing anything if I could help it. I was propping up a wall, cuddling

1

a whisky on the rocks, wondering when I could slip away when Henry Chandler came up to me.

Henry Chandler was alleged to be worth two hundred million dollars. His kingdom comprised computers, kitchen equipment and frozen foods. As a sideline, he owned the *California Times* and a successful Vogue-like glossy, selling fashions to the wealthy. He was the city's leading Quaker, his money had built the local, vast Quaker church and he was the least liked, most generous do-gooder of the city's rich citizens.

"Manson," he said, staring at me with his dark, hooded eyes, "I have been following your column. I like it. You have talent. Come and see me tomorrow at ten o'clock."

I went to see him and listened to his offer. He wanted to start a monthly magazine to be called *The Voice of the People* which would circulate throughout California: its purpose was to criticise and protest.

"This state," he said, "is riddled with corruption, dishonesty and crooked politics. I have an organisation that will supply all the information you will need so long as you feed them ideas. I'm offering you the job as editor because I believe you can handle this. I have had you investigated and I am satisfied with the report. You can choose your own staff. It can be small as the production and so on can be handled by my people working on my newspaper. You needn't worry about expenses. If the magazine flops, you will get two years' salary, but it won't flop. I have a brief here which I want you to examine. You will see you will have every support. Your job is to look for trouble. I'll take care of the libel suits. I have a top-class detective agency to work with you. We are not muck raking. I want you to be quite sure of that. There is no need to muck rake. We attack the administration, we attack police corruption and we go after the bribery and corruption boys. Does this interest you?"

I took his brief away and studied it. This was the most exciting thing that had ever happened to me. I talked it over with Linda and she was excited as I. She kept saying, "Thirty thousand!" Her lovely face alight. "We can at last move out of this godforsaken apartment!"

I had met Linda at a cocktail party thrown by an ambitious politician and had fallen in love with her. As I sat in the sun, I thought back to that moment when I first saw her. She was the most marvellous looking woman I had ever seen: she was blonde, beautiful, with big, marvellous eyes and a body that could only be the exact model of the perfect woman: heavy breasted, slim waist, solid hips and long tapering legs: a sex symbol *de luxe*. The fact that I was a society columnist and mixed with the best people appealed to her. She told me she thought I was heavenly romantic. She made a tiny living acting as one of the various hostesses who looked after an ambitious politician: mixing with his friends, supplying glamour to his background, filling them with whisky, but, so she assured me, strickly paws off.

We married within a week of our meeting. Our wedding night should have warned me. There was no passion, no nothing. She just gave herself, but I was hopeful to think that I could rouse her if I were patient enough: but I never did. I then discovered that her obsession was money. I was so crazy about her, I let her spend what I hadn't got. She was always buying things: handbags, clothes, costume jewellery, junk and because I wanted to keep her happy, I let her spend. She grumbled. She hated the small apartment in which we lived. She wanted a car. Why should she have to take a bus when I used the car for business? I loved her. I tried hard to jolly her along. I even showed her figures to prove we just couldn't afford the things she wanted. She wasn't interested. "You are famous," she said. "People always talk about you: you must be successful."

Just when I was really getting worried, this offer from Chandler arrived.

"I know just where we are going to live!" Linda told me. "Eastlake! It's marvellous! It has everything! Let's go tomorrow and pick a house."

I pointed out to her I hadn't got the job, hadn't made up my mind and beside, Eastlake was an expensive estate which could eat a hell of a hole in a thirty thousand dollar income.

This was our first real quarrel. I was startled by her

3

violence. She screamed at me and threw things. I was so shocked, I gave way. As soon as I promised I would take the job and would go with her to look at Eastlake, she came into my arms and apologised for being 'so naughty.'

So I went to Chandler and told him I would be his editor.

He sat behind his desk, looking like a vast blow-up of what a two hundred million dollar executive had to look like, a big cigar rolling between his thick lips.

"Fine, Manson, the contract is all ready." He paused and regarded me, his hooded eyes probing. "Now, one thing: you will be attacking the corrupt and the dishonest. Remember you will be a goldfish in a glass bowl. Be careful: don't give anyone any chance to hit back at you. Goldfish have no hiding place. Remember that. Take me: I am a Quaker and proud of it. I believe in God. My private life can't be criticised. No one can point a finger at me and no one must be able to point a finger at you. Do you understand? No drinking when driving: no fooling with women. You are respectably married so keep that way. No debts. No nothing the opposition can pin on you. You step out of turn and every newspaper in this state will come after you. You now have a mission to attack the corrupt and the dishonest and you are going to have a lot of enemies who will crucify you if they can."

Because I needed his thirty thousand dollars a year, I said I understood, but after signing the contract, after shaking his hand and when I left his opulent office and went down to my car, I had misgivings. I was already in debt: I had a bank overdraft. I had Linda who spent and spent.

But for all that, I stupidly let her talk me into buying a house at Eastlake.

Eastlake is a housing estate built for the upper income bracket people. The comfortable, *de luxe* houses sold around $75,000 and they were equipped with fitted carpets, dish washers, air conditioners, you name it it's there, even to a lawn sprinkler. These houses are built around an artificial lake of some two hundred acres. There is a Club house, riding, tennis, swimming, a golf course (floodlit at night) and a vast *de luxe* Self-service store that supplied anything from caviar to a pin.

Eastlake was Linda's idea of paradise. She had a number of friends living there. We just couldn't live anywhere else, she told me. So I bought a house with a horrifying mortgage that would cost me $10,000 a year in fees, property tax and outgoings.

We moved in and Linda was happy. The furniture took all my savings. I had to admit that the house was marvellous and I was proud to be the owner, but at the back of my mind, I kept thinking of the cost. We had neighbours; young people like ourselves, but I suspected the husbands were better off financially than I was. Every night we either entertained or were entertained. Linda, of course, wanted a car of her own. I bought her an Austin Mini Cooper. She was never satisfied. She wanted way-out gear: her friends were constantly changing their clothes, so why shouldn't she? She couldn't cook and hated housework so we had Cissy, a large black woman who came in her beatup Ford every other day and cost me $20 a visit. My $30,000 a year that had looked so good when I had signed Chandler's contract shrank to nothing.

But, at least, the magazine was a success. I had been lucky to find two top-class reporters, Wally Mitford and Max Berry, to work with me. Chandler's detective agency fed me with a stream of information. Chandler lent me his advertising expert who really knew his job. Financially, the magazine had no problems. With Mitford and Berry helping, I lifted the lid off a lot of corruption and consequently made a lot of enemies. This I had to accept. I went after the Administration and the politicians. After the fourth issue, I knew I was a hated man, but I kept strictly to facts and there was nothing anyone I attacked could do about it.

Sitting in the sun, taking stock, I saw how vulnerable I was if some enemy began to probe into my private life. I was burdened with a $3,000 overdraft. I was living beyond my means. I didn't seem able to control Linda's spending. If some columnist wanted to be spiteful he could hint that Linda and I were falling out and I knew that would upset Chandler whose married life was blameless.

In the next issue of *The Voice of the People,* due out at the middle of the month, I was attacking Captain John Schultz, the Chief of Police. I was raising inquiring eyebrows that he was able to run a Cadillac, live in a $100,000 house, send his two sons to the University and his wife wore mink. Chandler had told me to go after Schultz whom he hated. What I had written was the truth, but attacking the Chief of Police was asking for personal trouble. I knew, once the magazine was on the streets, I would have to be very, very careful: no parking offenses, no driving even after one drink: every cop in the city would be told to gun for me.

As I sat by the empty swimming pool, I wondered if what I was doing made sense. I hadn't Chandler's Quaker mentality. I was in this for the money. It was fine for him: he could take care of any libel action and he was a natural crusader: I wasn't.

Tomorrow was the first of the month. It would be the day of reckoning when I paid my last month's bills. I went over to my desk and spent the next two hours listing what Linda and I owed. The amount exceeded the quarterly payment from Chandler by $2,300. I analysed my outgoings. Apart from Linda's extravagance, the worst inroad was liquor and meat bills. When you entertain ten to fifteen people twice a week, providing them with vast steaks and unlimited liquor, you really ran away with the money, plus Cissy, plus the monthly payments on my car and Linda's car, plus living expenses and provision for income tax and property tax, I wondered I wasn't more in the red.

I sat back feeling trapped. I would have to do something, but what? The obvious thing was to sell the house and move into a small apartment in the city, but by now I was regarded as a big success by the people of Eastlake and could I afford to raise the white flag and quit?

The telephone rang. It was Harry Mitchell.

"Hi! Steve! Are you coming over? Do I put a steak on for you?"

I hesitated, looking at the litter on my desk. What was the point in sitting here, making sums?

"Sure, Harry, I'll be right over."

As I replaced the receiver, I thought tomorrow could bring a solution, although common sense told me it wouldn't.

I would have to talk to Linda and this was something I dreaded. I knew she would make a scene. I still vividly remembered our last major quarrel. But she had to be told. We had to cut down expenses. She had to co-operate.

I locked up the house, went to the garage and got in my car. I liked Harry and Pam Mitchell. He earned big money in real estate. I suppose he earned three times what I did. They never had less than thirty people to their Sunday Bar-B-Qs.

I drove over to his place, telling myself without any hope that tomorrow was another more hopeful day.

*   *   *

Jean Kesey, my secretary, was in my office, arranging my mail as I came in on this Monday morning.

A word about Jean: she was around twenty-six years of age, tall, dark with a good figure, a good face without being pretty and she was one hundred percent efficient. She had come from the Chandler stable, having worked for him as his fourth secretary and he had parted with her reluctantly, telling me he was making me a valuable present and a valuable present she was.

" 'Morning, Steve," she said, smiling at me. "Mr. Chandler wants you. 'As soon as he comes in, I want him.' His very words."

"Did he say why?"

"It's all right. I know by his voice. No trouble."

I looked at my watch. It was 09.08.

"Doesn't he ever sleep?"

She laughed.

"Not often . . . he's waiting."

So I went down to my car and drove over to the Chandler building.

His secretary, a middle-aged woman with eyes like the points of ice picks waved me to his office door.

"Mr. Chandler is expecting you, Mr. Manson."

7

Chandler was behind his big desk, reading his mail. He looked up as I came in, rested his bulk back in his executive chair and waved me to the visitor's chair.

"Steve, you've done a swell job. I've just read the proofs about Schultz. I think we've got this sonofabitch on the hot seat. It's well done."

I sat down.

"I could also be on the hot seat, Mr. Chandler."

He grinned.

"Sure . . . that's what I want to talk to you about. From now on, you're going to be a marked man. The cops will be told to hate you. They're scared of me, but not of you. I'm willing to bet Schultz will resign in a few weeks, but before he goes, he'll try to hit back at you. I want to take care of this." He paused to study me. "Have you any personal problems?"

"Who hasn't?" I said. "Yes, I have personal problems." He nodded.

"Nothing worse than money?"

"No."

"Sure? Level with me, Steve. You have done a damn fine job with my magazine. I'm on your side."

"It's just money."

"That's what I thought. That lovely wife of yours is running you into debt, isn't she?"

"I'm running myself into debt, Mr. Chandler."

"That's right. People these days over spend. They live beyond their means. Their wives compete with the other wives and it costs. Don't imagine I don't know the problem although it doesn't nor ever will happen to me. That article you wrote rates a bonus." He flicked a cheque across his desk. "Fix your debts, and from now on control your wife. She's a beauty, but no woman should be allowed to run wild."

I picked up the cheque. It was for $10,000.

"Thank you, Mr. Chandler."

"This mustn't happen again. Remember what I said: goldfish have no hiding place and you're living in a goldfish bowl. I'm bailing you out, giving you a new start, but if you can't control the situation from now on, you're not the man for me."

We looked at each other.

"I understand."

I drove to the bank and paid in the cheque. I talked to Ernie Mayhew, my bank manager. This cheque would clear my overdraft, take care of my debts and leave me with a decent credit balance. I left the bank, feeling like a man who has shifted a ton of cement off his back.

Although I had been determined to talk to Linda about our finances, we had stayed so late with the Mitchells, the opportunity didn't arise. We were both slightly drunk on our return and we flopped into bed. I had tried to make love, but she had moved away, muttering, "Oh, for God's sake . . . not now." So we had drifted off to sleep and she was still sleeping when I got up, made myself coffee and she was still sleeping when I left for the office.

The morning was spent putting the magazine to bed. I decided that because of the attack on the Chief of Police I would increase the printing order by 15,000 copies.

After a desk lunch, I settled down to plan the next issue. While I was planning, the thought that I would have to talk to Linda tonight kept creeping into my mind.

This mustn't happen again. I'm bailing you out. If you can't control the situation from now on, you're not the man for me.

I recognised this as a warning and I knew Chandler always meant what he said. So, tonight, I had to talk straight to Linda and she would have to accept the fact that we could not go on living at our present standards.

The coming battle—and it was going to be a battle—with Linda made creative thinking impossible. I shoved aside my chair, got up and began to move around my big office. I could hear the faint clack of Jean's typewriter. I also could hear Wally Mitford's voice as he dictated into a Grundig. I looked at my desk clock. The time was 16.15. I had two hours yet before I could go home and talk to Linda.

I lit a cigarette and moved to the big window that gave

me a view of the city. Smog made it necessary for the cars to turn on their headlights. I looked across at the Chandler building. The penthouse, where Chandler worked, was a blaze of lights.

The buzzer sounded. I walked over and flicked down a switch.

"There is a Mr. Gordy here, Mr. Manson," Jean told me. "He would like to see you."

Gordy? The name rang no bell.

"What does he want?"

There was a pause, then Jean said, her voice sounding a little troubled, "He says it is personal and confidential."

"Send him in in three minutes."

This would give me time to put a tape on the recorder, switch on the mike, settle myself behind my desk and light another cigarette.

Jean opened my door and stood aside as a tall, thin man, wearing a well worn, but neatly pressed suit, came into my office. He was around forty years of age, balding with a broad forehead, tapering down to narrow jaws, a thin nose, deep-set eyes and an almost lipless mouth.

I stood up to shake hands. His hand felt dry and hard.

"Mr. Gordy?"

"That's right. Jesse Gordy." He smiled and showed small yellow teeth. "You wouldn't know me, Mr. Manson, but, of course, I know you.'

I waved him to a chair.

"Please sit down."

"Thank you." He settled himself in the chair, took out a pack of Camels and lit up. There was something about his movements, his expression, his arrogant, confident ease that began to bother me.

"Was there something?" I moved some papers to give him the hint I hadn't time to waste.

"I think I have information for you, Mr. Manson, that would make an interesting article." He again revealed his yellow teeth in a tight smile. "I have been reading your magazine: quite first class: quite the thing this city needs."

"I'm glad you think so, Mr. Gordy. What is this information?"

10

"First, let me introduce myself. I am the manager of the Welcome Self-service store on the Eastlake estate. I don't believe you come to the store, but your wife shops with us I am happy to say." Again the lips lifted, again I saw the small yellow teeth: they began to make me think of a rat. "Every lady living at Eastlake shops with us."

I had a growing feeling that there was something menacing behind this smooth talk and I was careful to look interested, to nod encouragingly and to wait.

"Mr. Manson, you have created a splendid, vigorous magazine that attacks dishonest people. It is a fine, much-needed endeavour," Gordy said. "I have read all the issues and I look forward to reading the next." He leaned forward to tap ash off his cigarette into my glass ashtray. "I'm here, Mr. Manson, to offer you information concerning petty theft in my store. It is called petty theft, but over a year, the amount of stealing comes to some $80,000."

I stared at him.

"You mean people living on the estate steal $80,000 a year from your store?"

He nodded.

"That is correct. I don't know why it is, but people do steal: even well-off people. It is an oddity that, so far, hasn't been explained. A servant working on the estate will buy ten dollars' worth of goods and will steal two packs of cigarettes. A wealthy lady will buy a hundred dollars' worth of goods and yet will steal an expensive bottle of perfume."

This began to interest me. If what this man was telling me was true I could write an explosive article which Chandler would love.

"You surprise me, Mr. Gordy," I said. "You have proof?"

"Of course."

"What proof have you?"

He stubbed out his cigarette and lit another as he smiled at me.

"In spite of the heavy cost, my directors decided to install camera scanners that cover the whole store. The cameras began to operate two weeks ago. My directors consulted the

Chief of Police who expressed his willingness to prosecute
on the evidence the film produced, providing the film was
convincing." He relaxed back in his chair. "The film I now
have, Mr. Manson, is so convincing, I hesitate to hand it
over to Captain Schultz. I felt I should first consult you
and a number of husbands whose wives shop in my store."

I felt a sudden rush of cold blood up my spine.

"I'm not following you, Mr. Gordy," I said and heard
my voice was husky. "Just what do you mean?"

"Mr. Manson, please don't let us waste time. Your time
is precious and so is mine." He produced from his pocket
an envelope and flicked it on to my desk. "Look at this. It
is a blow-up from a frame of twenty feet of film. I suggest
it is enough proof, apart from the film, to tell you that Mrs.
Manson has been naughty."

I picked up the envelope and drew from it a glossy
photograph. It showed Linda, looking furtive, putting a
bottle of Chanel No. 5 into her handbag.

I sat still, like a stone man, staring at the photograph.

"Of course she isn't the only one," Gordy said gently.
"So many ladies of Eastlake do this kind of thing. The film
is very revealing. Captain Schultz would have no difficulty
in prosecuting. Your nice, beautiful wife, Mr. Manson,
could even go to prison."

Slowly, I put the photograph down on my desk.

Gordy got to his feet.

"This is, of course, a shock to you," he said, showing
his yellow teeth. "You will need time to think about it and
even discuss it with Mrs. Manson. We could arrange this
sad affair. Before I give Captain Schultz this revealing
cassette of film I could snip out your wife's participation. I
suggest $20,000 and you get the film. It is not a lot of
money considering your success. May I suggest you come
and see me tomorrow night with cash. I have a small,
modest house not so far from your beautiful house. No. 189
Eastlake." He leaned forward, staring at me, his eyes like
chips of ice, his yellow teeth now revealed in a snarl. "Tomorrow night, Mr. Manson . . . cash please," and he walked
out of my office while I sat there, staring at Linda's beauti-

ful face, seeing her doing this mean, mean thing and knowing I would have to save her from prosecution.

But how?

I had always told myself that if ever anyone tried to blackmail me, I would go immediately to the police: the only way of dealing with a situation like that. But my attack on Schultz would make this impossible for me to go to him. He would certainly stamp on Gordy, but he would have no mercy on Linda unless . . .

Could I withdraw the article? I still had over a week before the printing run. I had a lot of material I could substitute but Chandler had okayed the article. He had given me a bonus of $10,000, clearing my debts, for creating the article. Could I now persuade him that our facts might not stand up and we could get landed with a hell of a libel suit?

There was a tap on my door and Wally Mitford came in.

"Have you time to look at this draft about the new High school building, Steve?"

I wanted to be alone to think and it was an effort to say, "Sure. Sit down."

Wally took a chair and began spreading papers on my desk I slid the photo of Linda into my desk drawer and turned off the tape recorder.

Wally was tubby and amiable looking, around forty years of age. He had a receding hair line, eyes almost hidden behind thick lensed glasses and the jaw of a bulldog. He was the best research reporter I knew and I have met a lot of them.

We discussed the new High school which was being built by a contractor employed by the City Hall. Wally thought the estimate was far too high. He had inquired around and had discovered at least three other contractors who had put in a much lower bid.

"It's Hammond," he said. "He's getting a big rake off. We could start trouble for him. What do you think?"

"See what Webber can dig up about him."

Webber was head of Chandler's detective agency.

"Okay." Wally made a note. "Are you all right, Steve? You look as if you're sickening for the flu."

"Nothing more than a headache." I paused, then said, "That article about Schultz. Do you think we should run it?"

"Run it?" He gaped at me. "Are you fooling?"

"I've been thinking about it. It could land us in a lot of trouble. I mean the cops will really turn sour and it could mean personal trouble for us all."

"We talked that out when we planned the article, didn't we?" Wally grinned. "You planned it and I wrote it: so you and I are the boys out on a limb. What have we to worry about? What can the cops do to us? I, like you, behave myself . . . so what?" He regarded me. "Are you getting cold feet, Steve? Have you a secret past?" His wide grin did nothing for me. "Besides the boss has given us the green light. If there is any trouble he takes care of it and that sonofabitch Schultz has it coming."

"Yes. Okay. You talk to Webber and see what you can dig up about Hammond."

He gave me a thoughtful stare, gathered up his papers and started for the door.

"Take it easy tonight, Steve. Go to bed early."

When he had gone, I ran off the tape and put the *cassette* in my pocket. I put the photograph in my brief-case, then I went into Jean's office.

"I'm going home, Jean. I've got a chill or something. Wally will be here if anything turns up."

She looked with concern at me.

"Have you any Aspros at home?"

"Sure. I'll be fine tomorrow," and I went out into the corridor. Wally's office door was open. I looked in.

"I'm going home, Wally. If there's trouble, call me."

"There won't be. Have an early night."

I hesitated, but I had to know.

"Does Shirley shop at the Welcome stores?"

Shirley was Wally's nice, practical wife.

"That den of thieves?" Wally shook his head. "I reckon they are more than fifteen percent ahead of any other store in the district. It's just for the rich and the snobs. We could do an exposure on them, Steve. We could cut them down to size."

14

"It's a thought. Well, see you tomorrow," and I took the elevator down to the street level. I got in my car, started the motor and stared bleakly through the windshield.

What was I to do? Twenty thousand dollars by tomorrow night or this film would go to Schultz. I could imagine the police arresting Linda. I could imagine the sensation and how the press would love it. Chandler would immediately give me the gate. I thought of all our neighbours: the yak, the head wagging and for the first time since I married Linda, I was thankful we had no children.

But there must be a way out.

I had cleared my overdraft. Would Ernie Mayhew advance the $20,000? That, after brief consideration, I knew was a pipe dream. He might advance me $5,000 if I thought up some reasonable excuse. But how to raise the rest of the money? I thought of Lu Meir who lent money and who I was planning to attack. Max Berry, my other researcher, had alredy drafted a blueprint. We were going to attack Meir on his 60% interest loans and Max had details about Meir's collectors: thugs who beat-up those unfortunates who couldn't pay this exorbitant interest. Maybe if I killed the article, Meir would lend me the money at reasonable rates, but then I remembered Chandler had already seen Max's first draft and had approved it.

I shifted the gear stick to drive and headed for home.

*　　　*　　　*

Once out of the city and through the smog belt, the evening sun was hot and the air clear. I didn't expect to find Linda at home and I wasn't disappointed. The garage doors were open and the Austin Cooper not there. I drove my car into the garage, looked at my watch—the time was just after 18.00—then unlocked the door from the garage into the house and went to my study. I wound the tape onto my recorder, put the photograph in my desk drawer, then went into Linda's dressing-room. It took me only a few minutes to find the bottle of Chanel No. 5. I then opened her make-up cabinet and surveyed the bottles and lotions that lined the shelves. Any of these, of course, could have been stolen. There was a large, ornate bottle of Joy perfume. *The New Yorker* had told me in an ad. that this was the most expensive perfume you could give a woman. I closed the cabinet door and went into the kitchen to get ice for a drink I badly needed.

The kitchen was in a mess: our breakfast things stood in the sink, the remains of a Quick-lunch curry chicken cluttered the kitchen table with a used plate, knife and fork. Bread crumbs were scattered on the floor. I remembered that Cissy would arrive tomorrow. I went back to my study, fixed a drink and sat behind my desk. I sat there, trying to think up a solution. I admit to panic. I saw everything I had worked for, my whole future blown sky high because my stupid, beautiful wife had to be greedy. Why couldn't she have asked me to buy her perfume? How could she have been so utterly irresponsible as to turn thief, knowing if she were caught, what it would mean to both of us?

I forced my mind away from her and thought of Jesse Gordy. I thought back on what he had said, then not sure, I switched on the tape and listened to his voice.

The film I now have, Mr. Manson is so convincing, I hesitate to hand it to Captain Schultz. I felt I should first consult you and a number of other husbands whose wives shop in my store.

So, obviously, Linda wasn't the only thieving wife. Others of my neighbours were being blackmailed. My mind darted as I thought of the people we knew who lived around us. The Mitchells? The Latimers? The Thiessens? The Gilroys? The Creedens? The list could go on and on: all wealthy men with spoilt wives: much more wealthy than I was, but I doubted if their wives who I knew well were more spoilt than Linda. Could these husbands have received a visit from Gordy? Suppose there had been four other thieving wives? A demand of $20,000 a wife. $80,000 for a visit, a threat and a snippet of film!

I felt a sudden surge of anger and picking up the telephone receiver I called Herman Webber.

The Alert Detective Agency was owned by Henry Chandler and was run by Herman Webber. This man had been a police lieutenant, had resigned because his promotion wasn't rapid enough and had set up a private inquiry agency. He had been popular with the police and in next to no time, five top-class police officers had deserted the force and had joined him. Chandler had financed him and had now taken him and his five officers under his wing. Webber had done all the dirty research for *The Voice of the People*. I didn't like him: he was tough, hard and tricky to deal with, but he came up with facts and his facts stuck.

His hard, clipped voice came on the line.

"Webber."

"This is Steve, Herman," I said. "I have a little job that needs taking care of."

"Go ahead: you're being taped."

That was Webber: efficient and still the cop. He never took any assignment unless he had everything on tape.

"Jesse Gordy," I said. "He runs the Welcome Self-service store. I want everything about him: repeat everything about him down to how often he cuts his toenails and fast."

"Can do. No problem. I have a file on him that only needs bringing up to date. You'll have it by noon tomorrow."

"Make it ten o'clock."

He whistled.

"Like that?"

"I want it on my desk by ten o'clock," and I hung up.

I looked at my watch. The time now was 18.20. I looked in my address book, then called Ernie Mayhew's private number. Martha, Mayhew's wife, answered.

"Is Ernie back yet? This is Steve," I said.

"He's just taking a pee," Martha said and laughed.

"How are you both? It seems ages since we saw each other. When can we get together? How about next Friday? Do come along."

"Fine. I'll talk to Linda. You know how it is, Martha, the man never counts. She could have something on."

Martha squealed.

"Well, I hope so, Steve."

Then Ernie took over.

"Hi, Steve!"

"Look, Ernie, an emergency has come up. Linda's mother has to have an operation. Sorry to talk business at this time but I want to pour oil. Am I okay for $15,000?"

There was a pause.

"You don't mean you're asking . . ." Suddenly aware that Martha was listening, he stopped.

"That's what I'm asking. You can have the house for security, Ernie."

Again a long pause.

"Suppose we discuss this tomorrow, Steve? I'll make a date for nine-fifteen at my office."

"Can you give me some idea if you could or you couldn't?"

"We'll talk about it. I would say the amount isn't realistic. Anyway, let's talk. Sorry about Linda's mother."

"Yes."

"Let's get together, huh?"

"Sure. Okay. Ernie, tomorrow," and I hung up.

I heard Linda's Austin-Cooper as she drove into the garage. I flicked on my desk light, finished my drink and waited.

I heard the front door open and slam. She didn't bother to call out to me, but ran upstairs. I heard her heels thumping over my head as she crossed to the bathroom. There was a pause, then the toilet flushed. I sat there, waiting. The telephone bell rang. Although the receiver was just by my hand I didn't touch it.

I heard Linda, from our bedroom, take the call. I listened to her yakking.

"Steve! It's Frank." She had come out on the landing and was calling down. "He wants you."

I picked up the receiver.

"Hi, Frank!"

"How's about coming over in twenty minutes?" Frank Latimer asked. Listening to his deep baritone voice I wondered if his wife was a thief as mine was. "Sally has just bought a box of King size prawns. Jack, Suzy, Merrill and Mabel are coming. How's about it?"

Linda came into the study.

"Not tonight, Frank . . . thanks all the same," I said. "I've got a chill or something. I'm planning an early night." I listened to his commiseration, then hung up.

"Chill?" Linda was glaring at me. "What are you talking about? We haven't any food in the house! Call him back and tell him you have changed your mind!"

"It won't hurt us to starve," I said. "Sit down. I want to talk to you."

"If you don't want to go, I do!" She came over to my desk and reached for the telephone receiver as I took from my desk drawer the bottle of Chanel No. 5 and put it directly before her.

two

OFTEN ENOUGH, and sadly enough, there comes a moment of truth when a husband or a wife looks at his/her partner and realises he/she is no longer in love. That the months and even years they have lived together have turned suddenly into grey ash, and love—which is a precious thing—no longer exists between them.

This was my moment of truth as I watched Linda's hand hover over the telephone as she looked at the bottle of Chanel No 5. I watched her hand slowly withdraw and I watched the wary, sly expression come into her beautiful grey eyes. I watched her mouth set in a thin tight line, and for the first time since I had met her, I realised she wasn't as beautiful as I had thought she was.

When two people fall in love they have this thing that can never be replaced between them. It is a fragile thing: a wonderful thing, but it is fragile. Looking at Linda across my desk, this thing within me for her sparked out: the way an electric light bulb goes: one moment a bright light; the next moment darkness.

I waited, watching her. The tip of her tongue moved over her lips. She stiffened, then looked at me.

"What are you doing with my perfume?"

"Sit down, Linda. You've got us in a mess. Let's see if, between us, we can get out of it."

"I don't know what you're talking about." She had got over the shock and her voice was quite steady. There was now that bored look on her face she put on when she

21

thought I was being tiresome. "Call Frank and tell him we're coming."

"Does Jesse Gordy mean anything to you?"

She frowned.

"No. What's the matter with you tonight? Look, if you don't want to go, I'm going. I . . ."

"Gordy is the manager of the Welcome Self-service store. He came to me this afternoon and I took our conversation down on tape. Sit down. I want you to hear it."

She hesitated, then sat down.

"Why should I hear it?" But now her voice lacked her usual hard confidence. She eyed the recorder and I saw her hands turn into fists.

I pressed the playback button and we both sat motionless while Gordy's voice told its sordid tale. When he mentioned the photograph, I took it from my desk drawer and put it in front of her.

She took a quick look at it and her face became haggard. She suddenly looked five years older and when he said: *your nice, beautiful wife, Mr. Manson, could even go to prison,* she flinched as if flicked by a whip.

We listened to his voice to the end. *I suggest $20,000 and you get the film. It is not a lot of money considering your success. Tomorrow night, Mr. Manson . . . Cash please.*

I pressed the stop button and we looked at each other. There was a long, long pause, then she said, "What a goddamn fuss about a bottle of perfume. Well, I suppose you had better give him the money." She got to her feet. "It was stupid of me, but all the girls do it: why shouldn't I? As he said, considering your success, it is not a lot of money."

She started for the door. I don't think I have ever been so angry. I jumped to my feet, came around the desk and caught hold of her wrist as she was reaching for the door handle. I slapped her across her face so violently that if I hadn't been holding her wrist she would have fallen. As it was, she cannoned against the wall and went down on her knees. I jerked her upright and with a savage shove, sent her spinning into her chair. She landed breathless, her hand against her red, burning cheek and she looked hatred at me.

"You bastard!"

"And I could say ... you thief!"

"I'll divorce you for this! You hit me!" She was screaming at me now. "You've bruised me, you brute! God! How I hate you! I can't go out tonight! What will they say when they see me? Swine! To hit a woman! I'll make you pay for this! I'll make you sorry!"

I sat in my chair and watched her. She banged her fists on her knees. Her eye was beginning to swell. She looked silly and stupid: a spoilt, hysterical child showing off. Then suddenly she began to cry. She slid off the chair and came to me, falling on her knees, her arms around my waist, burying her face against my chest.

"Don't let them arrest me, Steve! Don't let them send me to prison!"

I had pity for her, but nothing else. Her clutching fingers could have aroused me to make love to her yesterday, but now they meant nothing to me.

"Linda! Get hold of yourself!" I could hear the hard note in my voice. "We have to work together on this. Come on! Get up! Sit down!"

She lifted her bruised, tear stained face, her hands moving away from me.

"You hate me, don't you, Steve? I suppose I deserve to be hated." She choked on her sobs. "But, Steve, get me out of this mess and I'll be a good wife to you. I'll ..."

"Shut up! Don't say things you'll regret later. Sit down. I'll get you a drink."

She got unsteadily to her feet.

"God! You're hard. I never thought ..."

She flopped in her chair.

I went to the liquor cabinet and poured two stiff whiskies. As I carried them to the desk, the telephone bell rang. I set down the glasses and picked up the receiver.

"Is Linda there?" A woman's voice.

"Linda is in bed with the 'flu. Who is it?"

"Lucilla. 'Flu? I'm so sorry. Anything I can do? You

23

have only to ask. I could come over. I'm marvellous at making soup."

Lucilla Bower lived in a bungalow at the far end of our road. She was a tall, rather ugly, middle-aged Lesbian who, I suspected, was far too interested in some of the wives on the estate.

"Thanks, Lucilla. No . . . we can manage."

"The poor dear. I could come over and hold her hand."

"Three Aspros are holding her hand at the moment. Anyway . . . thanks."

"Well . . . I mustn't keep you. I know how busy you always are. I do love your magazine, Steve."

"Fine. Well, good-bye for now," and I hung up.

Linda had finished her drink. I could see she was shivering and her eye was puffy. I poured more whisky into her glass.

"What are we going to do?" she asked. "God! You've hurt me! What are we going to do? Can you pay this bastard the money?"

I sat down and lit a cigarette.

"It's blackmail. Do you think we should?"

"Should?" Her voice went shrill. "He could send me to prison!"

"Would that scare you so much?" I regarded her. "After all there is proof that you are a thief and thieves expect to go to prison if they are caught."

"You're trying to frighten me! I won't listen to you! You hate me, don't you? You're mad about that two-faced secretary of yours. I know you have it off with her in the office. I know!"

I leaned forward and stared at her.

"Do you want me to hit you again? If you continue to talk like that, I will."

"Don't you dare touch me! I'll scream! I'll call the police! Don't you dare!"

I was sick of her and I was sick of everything.

"Go away, Linda. Let me think about this. Just leave me."

"I couldn't bear to go to prison! The disgrace of it!" She was crying again. "Help me! I didn't mean that about

Jean! I'm so frightened! I don't know why I did it . . .
they all do it!"

I couldn't bear this any longer. I had to think. I had to
be alone. I got up and left the room.

"Steve! Where are you going? Don't leave me!"

Her cry of despair only made me move faster. I left the
house, got in my car and drove off the estate. I passed the
luxury houses, seeing groups of people gathered around
their barbecues. I felt I wanted to drive off the rim of
the world and drop into oblivion.

* * *

The City Hall clock was striking seven as I drove into
my parking bay outside my office block.

I had to buzz for the nightman, Joey Small, who let me
in.

"Working late, Mr. Manson?"

"That's it."

My office was my only refuge: a place where I could
sit and think and try to come up with a solution. I travelled
up in the elevator, walked down the corridor and unlocked
my office door. As I entered, I heard the clack of a typewriter, coming from Jean's room.

I was surprised she was still working although I knew
from past experience she always left a clear desk before
going home. I had come to regard her with tremendous
respect and I knew that without her behind me *The Voice
of the People* wouldn't have been the success it was.

I switched on my office lights, then crossed over to her
door; opened it and looked in.

She was at her desk, her expert fingers flying over the
keyboard and she looked up, her eyes widening; her
typing stopped.

"I didn't mean to startle you," I said. "Aren't you
nearly through?"

"What are you doing back here, Steve?"

"I have things to think about."

"Wally has left me with a load, but I'm nearly through."

I looked at her, and for the first time I looked at her

as a woman and not as an efficient secretary and what I saw pleased me.

She was tall, dark and her eyes were serious and intelligent. For the first time I realised she had well formed breasts and nice hands. Her hair reached to her shoulders and was silky. She had a lovely throat.

"Is there anything wrong?" she asked. "You look ill."

I suddenly felt I could share this burden with her. I moved into her room, closed the door and wandered over to a chair by her desk.

"Linda has just told me that you and I are having it off in the office," I said as I sat down. I didn't look at her, but stared down at my hands.

"Why did she say that?" Jean's voice was quiet and gentle.

"I guess we've fallen out. She was thrashing around for an excuse to hurt."

"I'm sorry. Is there anything I can do?"

I looked at her. She was staring at me, her eyes worried and I could see she really wanted to be helpful.

"There's a lot more to it than that, Jean. I'm in a jam. I can't tell you about it. It's not my secret. Look, let Wally wait for his report. Get off. I want to be alone to think without the sound of a typewriter. Will you do that?"

"Have you eaten?"

"God, no! I couldn't eat a thing! I just want to do some thinking."

She stood up.

"Let's eat. I'm hungry. Then you can come back here and think as long as you like."

I realised this made sense. I was so goddamn tense I knew, unless I unwound, my thinking would be useless. And another thing: this would be the first time, since I had married, that I had taken a woman, except Linda, out to dinner.

"Wise girl. Let's go then . . . where?"

"Luigi." She snapped off her desk light. "Give me three minutes?"

I went back to my office, lit a cigarette and waited. My mind was empty. I was just thankful to have company and I refused to think of Linda with her black eye, alone in our expensive house.

Jean came in, putting on a light dust coat.

"We'll use my car," she said. "Let's go."

She drove me in her Porsche which had been a present from Chandler when she had left him to come to me. The traffic was heavy and parking was tricky. I realised it would have been a burden to me to have driven in my big Mercedes and she had taken this burden off my shoulders. Within ten minutes, she had found parking and we were entering Luigi's small, comfortable restaurant: a restaurant I never used for some reason or other, but I could tell at once that Jean used it a lot. At this hour, there were only three other couples: people I didn't know. Luigi, fat and beaming, brushed Jean's fingers with his lips, bowed to me and took us to a corner table.

"May I order?" Jean asked as we settled.

"I'm not hungry." I felt so low the idea of food revolted me.

Luigi stood over her, his little black eyes like oily olives.

"Oysters, Luigi, please: the big ones and Chablis."

She was right. Oysters were the only food I could have swallowed.

He went away.

"It's about Gordy, isn't it?" she said, looking directly at me.

I hesitated, surprised, then nodded.

"Blackmail?"

"How did you guess?"

"It's not so difficult. Wally has been researching. I've been typing his notes. When Gordy asked to see you, it became obvious."

"Wally's been researching?" I stiffened. "Does he know about Linda?"

"No. If he had he would have come to you. Wally admires you, Steve. He has a few names and he is still digging. Mostly maids: Cissy, your maid, is on his list."

I took out my handkerchief and wiped off my damp hands.

"Do you remember any names . . . not maids?"

"Sally Latimer. Mabel Creeden. Lucilla Bower."

The oysters arrived, bedded in crushed ice. The Chablis was poured. Luigi, officiating, beamed, then he and the waiter went away.

"How did Wally find out? How did he get those names?"

"I don't know. I typed up his report. There were other names, but I don't remember them."

"You're sure Linda wasn't on his list?"

"Of course."

"He said something about doing an exposure on the store. How is it he didn't tell me he had started?"

Jean speared an oyster and conveyed it to her mouth.

"You know Wally: he loves to spring a surprise. I guess he wanted to have it all tied up to present to you."

That I could accept. Wally was a loner. He had come up with facts and figures about Captain Schultz, all neatly tied up and I had had no idea he had been researching Schultz.

I found I could eat an oyster, so I ate three of them.

"Linda stole a bottle of perfume. Gordy has her on film. He wants twenty thousand dollars."

Jean drew in a quick, sharp breath.

"Which you haven't got." She was in the position to know as she handled my personal cheques.

"Which I haven't got. This could be my end and the end of the magazine. I've already told Webber to dig into Gordy's background. He could come up with something. It's my only hope. With luck, I could blackmail Gordy to stop blackmailing me."

"You'll have to be careful about Webber. He is Mr. Chandler's man."

"Yes. I must talk to Wally tonight."

"Why?"

"I have to find out where he got those names from. This is important."

"But, Steve, you know Wally. He never divulges his sources of information. You won't get anything from him."

"I got to try."

She nodded.

"Finish your oysters. I'll call his home. He could be in."

She slid off her chair and walked over to a telephone

booth. I looked at the oysters and decided I had had
enough. I watched her slim back as she telephoned. Three
minutes later, she joined me.

"He's just left. Shirley says he'll be back in an hour or
so. He's gone over to Max's place."

"You don't think he's told Max about this?"

"I'm sure he hasn't." She looked worried. "You know,
Steve, I'm breaking a confidence by telling you about what
Wally is doing. He told me to type up his notes in con-
fidence."

"This is too important to me to worry about that," I
said.

"Well, don't be surprised if Wally won't talk."

"He'll talk! He's got to!"

"You're not eating."

"I guess I've had enough."

"Steve! Eat up! This isn't the end of the world."

I thought of Linda with her black eye alone and without
food in the house. I shouldn't have left her.

"I want to make a call."

I went into the booth and called my home number.
There was a long delay, then a woman's voice said, "Mrs.
Manson is indisposed and Mr. Manson is out. Who is this?"

I recognised Lucilla Bower's drawling voice. Without
answering, I hung up. So Linda had quickly found com-
fort. I hoped she hadn't been so stupid as to tell this woman
what she had done, then I remembered that Wally had
Lucilla's name on his list as a thief. Well, thieves together!

I returned to the table.

"Let's have some more oysters," I said. "Nothing like
oysters for sick people."

"Oh, shut up, Steve!" Jean said sharply. "Don't start
pitying yourself. That's something I just won't take!"

I stared at her.

"You're quite a woman. Sorry: it's been a tough evening.
All the same I'd like some more oysters."

She looked across at Luigi and raised her hand. The
oysters arrived as if they had been waiting.

*　　*　　*

29

Forty minutes later, we left the restaurant and Jean drove me back to the office block. I had decided I should talk to Wally on my own. Jean said why not leave it until tomorrow, but if I could catch Wally tonight I had to go.

"Thanks for everything, Jean," I said. "You're a life-saver."

She stared at me for a brief moment, smiled, got in her car and drove away.

I drove fast across the city to where Wally lived: a modest, nice bungalow, but in the smog belt and nothing very *de luxe*. All the same, I was pretty sure Wally had a bigger bank balance than I had.

I pulled up outside the bungalow and was surprised to find it in darkness. I looked at my watch. It was just after 21.00. I got out of the car, opened the gate and walked up the drive. I rang the bell and waited. Nothing happened. I rang again, then a voice said, "They're not in."

I turned around. There was an elderly man with a dog by the gate.

"There's been trouble," the man went on. "Are you a friend of Mr. Mitford? I'm his neighbour."

I came down the path.

"I'm Steve Manson. Trouble?"

"I've read about you, Mr. Manson. Your magazine is just fine. Yes . . . trouble . . . poor Wally has been mugged. They've rushed him to hospital."

I felt a chill run up my spine.

"Is he bad?"

"I guess so. The police took him with Mrs. Mitford in an ambulance."

"Which hospital?"

"The Northern."

"Could I use your phone?"

"Of course, Mr. Manson. I'm right next door." He whistled to his dog and then led me up a path to a bunga-low just like Wally's.

In two minutes, I was speaking to Jean.

"Wally's hurt, Jean. He's at the Northern. Will you come over? Shirley will want help."

"I'll be right over," she said and hung up.

We both reached the Northern hospital at the same time. Jean had a little more distance to cover and she must have come fast. We looked at each other as she got out of the Porsche.

"Is he bad?"

"I don't know: let's find out."

I was lucky that Dr. Henry Stanstead was the doctor handling emergencies that night. Stanstead and I played golf together and we were friends.

"What's the verdict, Henry?" I asked as he came into the waiting-room.

"Bad. The bastards really set about him. He has a broken jaw, four ribs fractured and concussion: at least three kicks in the head."

"Shirley?"

He jerked his head to a door.

"In there. Look, Steve, I've got a busy night. Can you take her off our hands?"

"That's what we're here for." I turned. "Jean . . . will you?"

She nodded and went into the other room.

"He'll survive?"

"Yes, but he'll be bad for some days. He could lose an eye."

"The police?"

"I've told them there's no point hoping for a statement yet. Poor Wally won't be talking for at least four or five days."

Jean brought Shirley out and I went to her. She was crying and shaking.

"Shirley dear, I'm so sorry. I . . ."

She mopped her swollen eyes and glared at me.

"You and your filthy magazine! I warned Wally . . . he wouldn't listen to me!" She clung to Jean who looked at me, shaking her head.

I stood back and the two women went away.

"Okay, Steve, inquire as often as you like. He won't die." Stanstead patted my shoulder and hurried away.

Four or five days! I thought of Gordy. My one hope now was Webber. If he couldn't come up with something, I was sunk.

Slowly, I walked down the long corridor to the reception room.

"Manson . . ."

I paused, turned as a big, heavily-built man, wearing a slouch hat and a shabby raincoat came over to me. I recognised him as Sergeant Lu Brenner of the city police.

Brenner was pushing thirty-eight. He had a hard face, a flat nose, small restless blue eyes and he always looked in need of a shave: a powerfully-built man who I had heard had a reputation for cruelty. I had heard, but had no proof, that his method of interrogation was to hit first in vital spots and then ask questions. Webber had once told me that the only man in the world who meant anything to Brenner was Captain of Police, Schultz. Interested, I had asked why.

"You may not believe this, but this sonofabitch has a sweet wife. It so happened Mrs. Brenner was coming home when a junkie attacked her. He was high. Schultz—he was lieutenant then—saw the attack. He was too far down the street to be helpful. The junkie had a knife. So Schultz shot him. It was said it was the finest piece of marksmanship ever—an exaggeration, of course, but the slug passed under Mrs. Brenner's arm and spread the junkie's brains. She got a scratch from the knife. Brenner has never forgotten. He's been Schultz's man now for years and he stays that way."

I looked at Brenner.

"You want me?" I said, pausing.

"Yeah." He glowered at me. "This guy Mitford. We're interested. What's he been working on?"

"What's that to you?"

"Witnesses say Mitford got out of his car and two punks set on him. They beat him up and went off with a bulging brief-case. What we want to know is if this is a mugging or if someone is trying to stop him shooting his mouth off."

My mind worked swiftly. Wally had been working on the High school contract. He would certainly have the papers that could fix Hammond, but also he could have had his researching about the Welcome store which could involve a number of Eastlake's wealthy wives. This was something I wasn't going to tell Brenner.

"He was working on the High school contracts," I said. "The estimates are some fifty thousand dollars over the schedule."

He stared thoughtfully at me.

"That's City Hall business. Was there anything else?"

"Not as far as I know."

"I'd better talk to his wife. Has she gone back home?"

"I think so. Don't be too sure that because this is City Hall business, someone wouldn't want it hushed up."

He pushed his hat to the back of his head.

"Yeah. Well, if you snoopers stick your snouts out, you must expect to run into trouble."

"Can I quote you, Sergeant? Mr. Chandler could be interested to hear your views."

"Think so?" His eyes shifted. "Be careful you don't stick your snout out too far," and he walked away.

I wondered uneasily how he would react when he read the next issue of the magazine. Shirley would know of the planned attack on Schultz. If Brenner got to her, in her present hysterical mood, she could talk. I hesitated, then went to a telephone booth in the reception hall and called her number. There was no answer. I decided Jean could have taken her to her place and I dialled. Jean answered at once.

"Have you got Shirley there?" I asked.

"I've just got her to bed. I've given her two pills. She should sleep until tomorrow."

"The police want to talk to her, Jean. Keep her under the wraps. What was that about the filthy magazine?"

"She thinks Wally was attacked because of Hammond."

"Does she know about the Welcome?"

"I don't think so. She kept babbling about Hammond."

"Don't come in tomorrow until you have quieted her down. I don't want her talking to the police about the Welcome, Jean."

"I'll handle it. Suppose you call me around eight tomorrow morning?"

"I'll do that and thanks again."

I hung up and went down to my car. There didn't seem anything else I could do this night. Tomorrow, I would see Ernie Mayhew and try to raise some money. I'd go to the office and read Webber's report on Gordy. Everything now depended on him. If he failed me I would have to raise the money somehow.

I got back home around 22.15. No lights showed. Had Linda gone to bed? I hoped so. I was in no mood to cope with her right now. Unlocking the door, I went into the living-room, turned on the lights and looked around.

There was a sheet of notepaper lying on the table. I picked it up.

The letter said:

Dear Steve,
I am taking Linda to my place. Her eye should be all right in a couple of days, but in the meantime, to stop gossip, I will keep her with me.
Never hit a woman in the face. If you must hit her, slap her bottom. It has the same effect but the bruises don't show.

Lucilla

I crumpled the letter and tossed it into the trash basket. Then I made myself a drink and sat down.

It would seem I had a long, lonely night with panic edging my mind, ahead of me.

*   *   *

At 08.00 I telephoned Jean.

"How is Shirley?"

"She's fine. She's right here and wants to speak to you." A pause, then Shirley came on the line.

"Steve! I'm sorry I blew my tiny mind last night: please forgive me."

I drew in a long deep breath.

"There's nothing to forgive."

"I'll say there is! If Wally ever heard! He would kick me humpbacked! I just went crazy after seeing the darling.

34

God! They've hurt him!" Her voice broke. A pause, then she said, "The magazine is marvellous, Steve! Wally knew the risks and so did I, but when it came, I couldn't believe these animals could be so awful."

"I'm telling Chandler. He'll do something for Wally. He's going to be all right. It'll take a little time. I talked with Stanstead. You're not to worry." I didn't tell her Stanstead thought Wally might lose the sight of an eye. "Shirley . . . the police want to talk to you. Be careful what you say to them. No mention of Schultz. That bomb has to go off but not yet. Tell them Wally was working on the High school contract and nothing else . . . understand?"

"Yes, of course. Jean's been a darling. We're going over to the hospital right now."

"I'll be in touch."

"You do understand, Steve?"

"You're my girl. Would you give me Jean?"

Jean came on the line.

"I'm calling Chandler, then I'm going to the bank," I said. "I'll stick around the office until you come."

"Okay, Steve."

I called Chandler's home and just caught him as he was leaving for his office. I told him what had happened and that I suspected it was because of the High school contract that Wally had been beaten up.

Chandler rose to the occasion as I knew he would.

"Where is he?"

"The Northern."

"All right, Steve, I'll take care of it. I'll get a report on his condition. Tell his wife I'll take care of everything and I mean everything. His salary is to be doubled from yesterday. If these punks think they can intimidate me they have another think coming! Go after Hammond with no holds barred . . . understand?"

Yes, I understood, but Chandler wasn't in the firing line. My turn could come. I, too, could be in the Northern with broken ribs and concussion.

"Okay, Mr. Chandler. If you could have a personal word with Shirley?"

"Personal word? I'm going to the hospital right away and

I'll see her." A pause, then he said, "This mag of ours is certainly stirring them up, isn't it?"

"I guess it is." I thought of Schultz.

"Keep it up, Steve," and he hung up.

I made myself coffee, then drove over to Lucilla's bungalow. She answered my ring: a tall, gaunt woman with a mannish haircut, green, cold eyes and pinched nostrils. She had on shirt and slacks and she looked what she was: a bull dyke.

"Hello, Steve, come in. Our poor invalid is still sleeping."

I followed her into the big lounge, carelessly furnished with no pieces that matched, but comfortable and cluttered with books. She made a living writing articles for art magazines and reviewing books for the *California Times*. Chandler seemed to think a lot of her.

"How is she?"

"A black eye."

"She told you why?"

Lucilla nodded.

"Some women do stupid things."

"Twenty thousand dollars makes stupidity expensive."

"It depends. It could be cheap. Both of you would have to leave here and you would lose your thirty thousand a year job."

"You could also have to leave here. Chandler wouldn't go along with a thief."

She gave a soft chuckling laugh.

"I have my tiny bit of film. It cost me two thousand. I beat the creep down. He wanted five, but we settled for two."

"How do you know he hasn't kept some frames back?"

"Why should he? It's easy money." She laughed again. "I rather admire him. So many of us on the estate do it. Why shouldn't he horn in?"

"Two thousand is a little different from twenty thousand."

"Gordy's bright. He judges his customers. After all, Linda looks rich. I don't." She regarded me, her green eyes mocking. "You are rich, aren't you, darling?"

I moved to the door, asked, "Are any of the other husbands paying?"

She shrugged.

"How would I know? I do know no other husband has hit his wife."

"Maybe that is a pity," I said and left her.

At least I now had a little information. This woman had said she had bargained with Gordy: could I do that? This would have to be fixed with Gordy before the Schultz article appeared. Once Gordy knew about that, he could up his price.

I drove to the bank.

"Sit down, Steve," Mayhew said. "You're busy. I'm busy, so let's get down to it. I've looked into the situation. The best I can do is to fix a five thousand overdraft. Would that be any good to you?"

"Can't you make it ten, Ernie? This is an emergency."

"Sorry. I'm bending over backwards, advancing you five. I don't run this bank. I have three directors breathing down my neck."

"Could I raise money on the house?"

"You have an up-to-the-hilt morgage already . . . not a hope."

I forced a grin.

"Well, thanks, Ernie, I'll accept the five."

"I wish I could do more. Is Linda's mother bad?"

"I guess so."

Looking at him, as he gave me a sympathetic smile, I wondered if his wife, Martha, shopped at the Welcome store and if she was also a thief.

I reached my office, said hi! to Judy who worked the switchboard. She told me Jean hadn't come in yet. I said I knew about it and went into my office.

My last hope was Webber. If he failed me, I would have to go to Lu Meir and borrow at sixty per cent.

I went through my mail, then Webber called.

"One hell of a thing has happened," he said in his hard, cop voice. "My office was broken into last night and ten of my files were stolen. The Gordy file was among them."

My fingers gripped the receiver until my knuckles turned white.

"Can you remember what was in his file?"

"Look, we have fifteen thousand confidential files here. Jack Walsh put Gordy's file together eight months ago. He left us last month. I only read files when I have to."

Was there something in the tone of his voice that hinted that he was lying?

"Where's Walsh?"

"I wouldn't know. He was a drip and I got rid of him. Anyway, what's the interest in Gordy? Is he something important to you?"

"What do the police say about the break-in?"

He gave a rumbling laugh.

"I haven't reported it. They love me like cancer. What's the use, anyway? It was a professional job and the missing files aren't important."

"Then why were they stolen?"

A long pause, then he said, "I've told Mr. Chandler. He says let it go and leave the cops out of it."

"That doesn't answer my question. You've lost ten files. At least one of them must be important."

"Some nut. Look, I'm up to my eyeballs with work. Suppose you take it up with Mr. Chandler if you feel that curious," and hung up.

I replaced my receiver, thought for some minutes, then I dialled Webber's number again.

The girl said, "The Alert Detective Agency."

"This is Truman and Lacey, solicitors. I understand Mr. Jack Walsh worked for you. He is a beneficiary of a will. Could you give me his address?"

She didn't hesitate.

"I'm afraid you are mistaken. No one of that name has ever worked here."

I replaced the receiver. I knew now for certain that Webber had been lying to me.

three

WITH A knock on the door, Max Berry, my other re-searcher, came in. Max was a big husky, around thirty years of age with a rather flattened face, having been a keen boxer at his university. He wasn't quite in the same class as Wally as a researcher, but he was good and as tenacious as a terrier after a rat. He dressed carelessly, wearing baggy, hairy suits and a red tie that always managed to work its way toward his left ear.

"This is a hell of a thing about Wally," he said as he shut the door.

"It certainly is. Sit down." I was still coping with the shock that Webber was no longer on my side. Quite why, I hadn't time to think. My immediate reaction was his wife, Hilda, had also been robbing the Welcome store. That could be the only explanation: anyway as first thoughts.

"I've just come from the hospital," Max went on, drop-ping into a chair. "Sweet grief! They certainly worked him over! How I wish it had been me! Poor Wally isn't equipped for that kind of trouble. I'd have given those punks something to remember me by." He ran his fingers through his mop of black hair. "Any ideas, Steve? Do you think Hammond is behind this?"

"Could be." And Hammond could be, but I was so close to the Welcome store, I couldn't get it out of my mind. "I don't know. It could be mugging."

"I don't think so. Wally had a brief-case stuffed with trouble. He's a cagey sonofagun. He came to me last night and we went over the Hammond estimates, but I got the idea, only half his mind was working on it. I have the feeling he was onto something else that's now landed him in hospital. Did he confide in you?"

I moved my pen from right to left. Wally and I had always been close. I could trust him with any personal confidence, but I wasn't sure about Max. He was like a bull that rushed in, tossed its horns and if anyone got caught it was just too bad so long as he got a sensational story. I could imagine his reaction if I told him what had been going on at the Welcome store. He would probably charge down there and try to bludgeon Gordy to talk.

"You know Wally," I said cautiously. "He kept everything close to his chest. I think Hammond fixed him."

"That's my thinking. We have nearly all the facts. Wally was after a photocopy of the contract Hammond signed. We talked about it last night. I offered to get it, but he said he would get it. He has better contacts than I have." He leaned forward, staring at me, his dark eyes sombre. "I'll get it now."

"You know this article about Schultz," I said. "It was Wally's special thing. It's all tied up and in proof. I've been thinking about it. Look, Max, what happened to Wally could happen to you and me. My thinking tells me that we should drop the Schultz article until we have handled Hammond. We could need police protection, and if we publish this article about Schultz that's the last thing we're going to get."

He rubbed his flat nose with his thumb.

"Police protection? How can they protect us?"

"They can give us gun permits. Chandler could swing that."

He grinned.

"I don't need a gun." And he looked down at his big hands now into fists.

"Three toughs could take care of you, Max. You're not Superman."

He shrugged.

"Okay. I'll leave it to you. I'm going after Hammond." He got to his feet. "I'll be in after lunch," and he left.

I looked across the smog and saw the lights were blazing

in Chandler's penthouse office. I hesitated for only a moment. This could be the means of relieving pressure.

I called Chandler's secretary.

"Could I come over?" I said. "I want an important word with Mr. Chandler."

"Hold it."

A pause then she said, "If you will come right away. He's due off for Washington in an hour."

I got over there—you could call it dangerous driving—in five minutes.

Chandler was at his desk, a stuffed brief-case by his feet, a dust coat and his hat on a chair.

"What is it, Steve?" he said as I came in. "I'm just off. I've a session with the President. I could have something for you when I get back."

Carefully choosing my words, I explained that in view of the attack on Wally, and because I thought the attack could have come via the City Hall with Hammond behind it, I thought we should hold back our attack on Schultz.

"Once that article is printed, we will get no support from the police," I concluded. "Right now, we need their support if we're to find out who was behind the attack. Also, Mr. Chandler, this could happen again. I can't produce your magazine from a hospital bed. I want a pistol permit and one for Berry. This could turn into a fighting war. Unless Schultz co-operates, we could be in bad trouble."

Chandler regarded me from under his hooded lids.

"Have you anything to replace the Schultz article?"

"A mass of good stuff. I would run the facts on the new birth pill."

A pause, then he nodded.

"I hate letting that sonofabitch off the hook, but what you say makes sense. Okay, drop it from this issue. Maybe next month, huh?"

"Yes."

Again he regarded me.

"So you think Hammond was behind this attack on Wally?"

"It looks like it."

His secretary put her head around the door.

"Your car is waiting, Mr. Chandler."

"Tell Borg to fix pistol permits for Steve and Berry. Tell him to get them automatics." Chandler got to his feet. "We'll talk this over when I get back." This to me.

I helped him on with his dust coat. His secretary picked up his brief-case.

As we walked from his office, he asked, "How's Linda?"

I wondered how he would react if I told him I had given her a black eye. Instead, I said, "She's fine, thank you."

We moved onto the long corridor.

"I hear Webber had a break in last night," I said casually. "He has lost some files."

The great man didn't break his step.

"Yeah . . . some nut." He glanced my way. "Something in it?"

"I wouldn't know. I thought it odd Webber didn't call the police."

"The police? What use are they?" I could see his thoughts were far away. He was probably rehearsing what he was going to say to the President.

He reached the block of elevators. A little man took the brief-case. He didn't exactly drop on his hands and knees and bang his head on the floor, but he conveyed that impression.

"See you, Steve." Chandler punched me lightly on my shoulder. "We'll talk," and he strode into the elevator.

His secretary and I watched him and the little man descend out of sight. Then she gave me a curt nod and walked back to her office.

I went over to another elevator and thumbed the button.

*   *   *

As I entered my office, Jean was by my desk, sorting through the mail I had already read.

"Hi, Jean! How's Shirley?"

"She's making out. Wally is still in a coma, but they

don't seem worried about him. Shirley is back home. And Linda?"

"She's in good hands." I went around my desk and sat down. I looked at her. Standing near me, upright, a bunch of letters in her hand, she looked very capable. She was wearing a grey and white dress that suited her. Her dark hair was blossy. For the first time I noticed she was wearing a white gold watch with a white gold bracelet. I suddenly realised I was noticing things about her that were new to me: like her watch, the cut of her dress, the silkiness of her hair, like her calm, intelligent eyes.

A pause while we looked at each other, then she said, "Do you want to go through the mail now?"

"I've been through it. There's nothing you can't handle." I hesitated, then said, "Sit down. The day's started badly. Feel like listening?"

She put the letters on my desk and sat down.

"Badly?"

I told her about Webber's telephone call, that Mayhew couldn't advance me more than five thousand. I told her about my brief talk with Lucilla Bower, that she had told me she had beaten Gordy down and had paid for the damaging strip of film. I went on to tell her I had persuaded Chandler to drop the Schultz article and to give Max and myself pistol permits.

She listened, her face tense.

"Well, that's it," I concluded. "The door looks shut. I can't understand Webber. It could be his wife has been stealing and he is laying off Gordy. Chandler, of course, is too busy to bother. If Webber told him the files meant nothing and some nut broke in, why should Chandler think otherwise? But this really bothers me, Jean. I imagined I could rely on Webber. Now I can't. It looks as if I've got to raise fifteen thousand dollars somehow to keep Linda out of this mess."

"Why not try to stall Gordy?" Jean said quietly. "So far, you've gained time: gain some more time." She pointed to the telephone. "Call him and tell him you must have more time to pay. You could still come up with something that could fix him."

"Without Webber on my side, I can't see how I can."

"Perhaps Gordy's file is still in Webber's office. I could get at it."

I stared at her.

"What do you mean?"

"I once did Mavis Sherman, his secretary, a great favour. She will do anything for me. Try to persuade Gordy to wait a couple of days."

I picked up the receiver and asked Judy to get me Jesse Gordy of the Welcome Self-service store and then I hung up.

"How did you help Mavis Sherman?" I asked.

She shook her head.

"That's not your business, is it, Steve? So many people, these days, get into trouble. When I can help, I help." She lifted her hands and dropped them into her lap. "One day—who knows?—someone could help me."

The telephone bell rang.

"Mr. Gordy on the line, Mr. Manson," Judy told me.

"Mr. Gordy?"

"Yes, Mr. Manson. How are you?" The sneer in his voice was unmistakable.

"I will have to postpone our little transaction. In two days, there will be no problem, but right now there is a problem."

"Is that right? I too have problems. Let us discuss our joint problems tonight as arranged at nine o'clock. You remember the address: 189, Eastlake? A token could make me reasonable," and he hung up.

Jean had been listening in on the extension. We both looked at each other as we replaced the receivers.

"I'll take Mavis to lunch," she said, getting to her feet. "The birth pill article is in proof. I'll get it down to the printers."

The telephone bell rang. It was Marvin Goodyear who wrote our travel page. From then on until lunch time I hadn't a minute to think of my own problems. I had lunch with Jeremy Rafferty, our film and theatre critic. Not paying much attention, I half listened to him expound while we ate the business man's lunch. Every now and then, he would pause in his monologue—Jeremy was a non-stop talker—and regard me. Finally, he said, "I get the idea I'm not making an impact, Steve. Are you sickening for something?"

"I've got Wally on my mind," I said, which wasn't true. He shook his head.

"A terrible thing. Some muggers after drug money. It could happen to any of us. Now, look, suppose I do a piece about the danger of our streets, hooking it up with the violence of films?"

"Sure. Send me an outline." I waved to the waiter for the check.

"Man! You sound as enthusiastic as a dowager of eighty offered sex."

As I paid the check, I said, "What do you know about the sex lives of eighty-year-old dowagers?"

He laughed, thanked me for the lunch and took himself off. I drove over to my bank and presented a cheque for three thousand dollars. The teller beamed at me, said how much he liked the last issue of *The Voice of the People,* then excused himself as he disappeared into Ernie Mayhew's office. Ernie must have given him the green light for he came back and paid out three hundred crisp ten-dollar bills. I put them in my bill fold and drove back to the office, wondering if three thousand dollars would be Gordy's idea of a token payment.

Jean was still at lunch. I called the hospital and was told Wally was still in a coma. I then called Lucilla.

"The poor darling is feeling very low," Lucilla drawled. "I don't think it would be considerate to get her out of bed to talk to you. Her eye is quite bad."

"Then let us be considerate," I said and hung up.

Jean came in.

"I think I've got it fixed. Unless Gordy's file has been destroyed. Mavis will give us a photocopy. She says there was no break-in last night. As soon as Webber leaves, she'll check the files."

"When does he leave?"

"Around 19.00. Mavis has the keys. She'll telephone me as soon as she gets it."

"If I can get it before I see Gordy, I could have a lever."

"If it's there, you'll get it."

"Thanks, Jean. I've got three thousand dollars for Gordy. I called the hospital."

"So did I and I talked to Shirley. She's bearing up. She tells me Brenner has been to see her. She gave nothing away. Brenner now thinks it was a mugging."

"It could just possibly be."

"Well, to work. You have the leader to write, Steve. My desk is loaded."

When she had gone, I pulled my I.B.M. Executive to- wards me. The leader was about the dollar devaluation. I was in no mood to write sense, but somehow, after littering the floor with crumpled paper, I got something down on paper that did make sense.

The rest of the afternoon rushed away with telephone calls, three contributions with ideas, two bad, one good. While I was dictating to my Grundig, the intercom buzzed. I flicked down the switch.

"Mr. Borg is here, Mr. Manson," Judy told me.

Joe Borg was Chandler's dog-of-all-work. He handled anything that was tricky and I knew him to be a top-class man with a salary that made my thirty thousand a year peanuts. But he had a hell of a job that would have given me ulcers.

"Send him in."

Borg breezed in. He was short, thin, dark, around forty years of age. His eyes were like tiny black buttons and his mouth wore a perpetual grin.

"Hi, Steve!" He closed the door and coming to my desk, he put down a square carton. "Armaments for you and Max. There are pistol permits and two boxes of slugs." He eyed me. "Don't go killing people, Steve."

"That's quick work, Joe. Thanks."

"When the boss says so, it is so." Again he eyed me. "Watch it, buddy. Don't shoot until you see the whites of their eyes." He screwed his face into a comical grimace. "Now who said that?" He started for the door. "I've got a date with a hot piece of tail who cools fast if she's kept waiting," and he was gone.

46

I took from the carton two .38 police automatics with shoulder holsters and two boxes of cartridges. The permits were made out in my name and Max's name. I stood up, took off my jacket and put on the shoulder holster. I had been in the Vietnam war and I knew about guns. I checked the automatic, found it worked well, then loaded the gun. One thing I was determined about, it wouldn't be my fault if I landed up in hospital.

I put the gun in the holster, stood away from my desk and did five experimental draws. The gun came from the holster each time smoothly and fast. Satisfied, I took off the holster and put the set-up in my desk drawer. Then I called Max at his home address. There was no answer. Max lived on his own. He was one of those me who didn't want to be tied to one woman. He flirted around and was happy that way.

As I replaced the receiver, Jean came in.

"Mavis has just telephoned . . . no luck. Gordy's file has gone missing."

I sat behind my desk.

"Can you make sense of this, Jean? Webber told me he had a file on Gordy. Now this lie about a break-in: now no file."

"I can only guess. Either he is being blackmailed by Gordy or someone with influence has persuaded him to lay off."

"Who?"

She thought, frowning.

"Who has been stealing from the store?" she asked finally. "According to Wally, Sally Latimer, Mabel Creeden and Lucilla Bower. I don't know any of these women. Do you?"

Mark Creeden immediately jumped into my mind. He owned the biggest house on the Eastlake estate. He was the President of the Howarth Production Corporation: a big wheel, the most important man on the estate. His wife, twenty years his junior, was inclined to act regally, as he did, and the women on the estate didn't go for her, including Linda.

Creeden had enough pull and enough money to put

47

Webber in his pocket. But why should he want Gordy's file destroyed? What could be in it to cause a man like Creeden trouble? Thinking about it, I decided I liked Webber better for being anxious to keep Gordy under cover. It could be his wife, Hilda, had been stealing.

I lifted my hands and let them drop on my desk.

"I'll see Gordy tonight. Maybe I'll get an angle." I looked at my watch. The time was 19:15. "Have dinner with me, Jean."

"Thank you, but I have things to do at home."

I so badly wanted her company.

"Oh, come on. Let's go to Luigi again."

She looked steadily at me, her dark eyes remote.

"Don't you think you should see your wife?" There was a tiny emphasis on the word 'wife' that wasn't lost on me. "I'll be home. Call me after you have seen Gordy," and she was gone.

She was right of course. I had no claim on her, married as I was to Linda.

I waited until I heard her leave the office, then after a moment's hesitation, I put on the shoulder holster, again checked the gun, turned off the lights, locked up and went down to the Eat's bar across the street for a lonely, depressing dinner.

*   *   *

It was 20.10 as I walked over to my car. I planned to drive home, see if there was any mail, get out the plan of the estate and locate Gordy's house, then go and see him.

"Hi, Steve!"

I turned.

Harry Mitchell was leaning out of the window of his Jaguar. He was two or three years older than myself: a big, rangy man with a pleasantly ugly face. He was a top class golfer and popular at the Country club.

I crossed over to his car.

"Sorry about Linda's mother. Is she bad?"

For a moment I didn't know what he was talking about, then I remembered I had told Ernie Mayhew the reason why I wanted money fast was because Linda's mother needed an emergency operation. Ernie must have told his wife and she had passed on the news.

"Not so good."

"Pam has been trying to get Linda. We guessed she's upped and left you to look after her mother."

"That's it. She shouldn't be too long."

"Can't have you being lonely, Steve. Come and join us tonight."

"Thanks, Harry, but this gives me the chance to catch up with my backlog."

He grinned.

"That's something I never get the chance of doing. If Pam's mother got ill and Pam had to go off, I guess I'd finally clear my desk." He laughed. "The old trout hasn't been ill for fifty years. Why not look in anyway?"

"I won't, Harry."

"Got over the 'flu?"

"Sure: short and sharp."

"When you call Linda, give her our love. How's about tomorrow night?"

"Let's see how it goes, huh?"

"Sure. You're doing a fine job on that mag. Even I read it." He waved and drove away.

I drove home. Cissy had been in. She had cleared up the kitchen and flicked dust around. I found the afternoon mail on the table. Most of the mail was for Linda who loved writing letters.

I decided it was an excuse to go over to Lucilla's place. I still had time before I saw Gordy. I dug out the plan of the estate. Gordy's house was tucked away at the end of East avenue. I decided I would walk there. There was no point in anyone seeing my car outside his place.

I found wearing the gun uncomfortable so I took it off and dropped the gun and the harness on the settee. Then I drove over to Lucilla's place. She opened the door.

"Surprise . . . surprise: here's the wife beater," she said with a cynical smile.

"I want a word with Linda."

"She's in the living-room. I'm cooking dinner: sorry I

can't invite you: there's only enough for two. Go ahead, Steve," and she went away.

I walked into the living-room. Linda, in a nightdress and wrap she had borrowed from Lucilla, reclined on the settee. Her eye was bandaged. She regarded me stonily with her other eye.

"Here are some letters for you." I dropped the letters by her side. "To try to raise the blackmail money I told Mayhew I needed money fast because your mother had to have an emergency operation. The news has spread as it always does on this goddam estate. Right now, you're supposed to be with your mother in Dallas."

"Must you have dragged mother into this?" Her voice was shrill.

"I'm seeing Gordy tonight. I have only been able to raise three thousand dollars. He'll want more, of course, but he might just wait. If he won't wait, I am going to sell your car and the jewellery I've given you and anything else we have that could fetch money."

Her one eye flashed and her mouth turned into a thin line.

"You don't touch my car nor my jewellery! They belong to me!"

I looked down at her. I couldn't understand how I had ever been in love with her.

"I'll see you after I have talked to him. We can then decide. You may, of course, prefer to go to prison."

As I started towards the door, she said viciously, "I hope that Kesey bitch is taking care of you."

"Don't make yourself more hateful than you already are," I said and went back to my car.

As I reached my house, I saw a car parked outside.

"Hi, Steve! I was wondering where you had got to." Frank Latimer came out of the shadows as I pulled up.

Latimer was a successful insurance broker. He was around forty years of age, balding, pot bellied but good fun.

"I heard the news about Linda's mum and I thought, as I was passing, I'll see if you felt like joining us for dinner. Sally has been on a shopping spree so we're eating late."

"Thanks, Frank. I've already eaten. I've got a whale of a lot of work to do."

"Yeah . . . I can imagine. That mag. of yours is just dandy. Well, I thought I'd stop by. If there's anything we can do . . ."

"It's all under control. Linda will be back soon and Cissy is looking after me."

"You know where we are if you want us."

When he had driven away, I put my car in the garage. According to Wally's report which Jean had told me about, Sally, Frank's wife, had been stealing. I wondered if Gordy had put the bite on him and if he was going to pay or had paid.

I looked at my watch. The time was 20.50: time I went to see Gordy. I locked up the garage, then walked down the avenue, passing the lighted windows of my neighbours, hearing the sound of television sets and wondering how Gordy would react when I offered him only three thousand dollars.

Turning to my right brought me to East Avenue. According to the plan of the estate, Gordy's house was some two hundred yards at the far end.

I quickened my pace. The avenue housed the cheaper villas on the estate and was not all that well lit. I came suddenly on a figure who emerged from shadows, a spaniel dog at his heels. I recognised Mark Creeden: a tall, heavily-built man in his early sixties.

Creeden was regarded by those living in Eastlake as the Czar of the estate. He was nearly as wealthy as Chandler and his house, I knew, cost four times the amount I had paid for mine. He ran a Rolls Corniche and his wife, Mabel, a Bentley T. Although both of them were a little regal, they entertained so lavishly, they were popular, but not really liked.

He stopped and peered at me. His over-red face creased into his wide, rather patronising grin.

"Hello, Steve! What are you doing out here?"

"Taking a walk to solve a problem," I said, wishing I hadn't run into him.

"Nothing like a walk to solve a problem. I'm exercising the dog. Mabel buys him and I have to do all the work." He laughed his jolly laugh: the sort of laugh ambassadors use to get a party going. "When are you two nice people coming to see us?"

"I guess when we are invited. Right now, Linda is in Dallas. Her mother is sick."

"Is that right? I'm sorry. There's a lot of illness around. So you are on your own?"

"Gives me a chance to catch up with my work."

"That's a fine magazine you're producing, Steve. I read every word. I won't keep you. I'll get Mabel to give you a call. We should see more of you both." More ambassador's talk. He bent to pat the spaniel. I thought it was a pity there were no press photographers to register the scene. " 'Bye now, Steve." He waved his hand as if leaving on a train and walked on.

I stared after him.

A coincidence?

First, Frank Latimer: now Mark Creeden. According to Wally, both these men's wives had been stealing from the Welcome store.

I wondered if Creeden had just left Gordy. Had he paid blackmail money to buy a strip of damaging film?

I moved on. I had some trouble finding Gordy's small two-storey house. It was well off the road. About two hundred yards from the rear of the house was the goods entrance to the Welcome store. The big store was in darkness, but there was a light showing through the yellow curtains of the lower room of Gordy's house. The rest of the house was in darkness.

I walked up the path, lined by straggly rose bushes. I pressed the bell. Chimes sounded, then died away.

I was sweating slightly and my hand felt cold and clammy. My heart was beating with an uneven thump-thump-thump. I knew I was doing a crazy thing to come here and pay money to a blackmailer, but the alternative of going to the police, even though the article on Schultz had been shelved, was too dangerous for Linda: too dangerous for me too. This stupid, greedy thieving could leak back to Chandler, and then there would be a full stop to my career.

There was no answer to my ring, so I rang again. I looked down the short, dark path, uneasy that someone could be watching me.

When again there was no answer, I hesitated, then put my hand on the door handle, turned and gently pushed. The door swung open. I stood there, looking into a small lobby. The light coming from the living-room—the door was ajar—showed me a coat rack on which hung a shabby dustcoat and a shabbier hat.

Anxious not to be seen by any passer-by, I moved into the lobby and closed the front door.

I wondered if Gordy lived alone. I wondered if he had a wife and if she knew he was a blackmailer.

"Gordy?"

I slightly raised my voice and waited.

I heard the sound of a refrigerator start up, but otherwise there was silence.

"Gordy?"

I moved to the door, tapped, then pushed it wide open.

How often have I read of this scene in books and seen it on television?

The shabby room with its fading, sun-bleached wallpaper, the ugly furniture, well used and much travelled, the cheap, well-worn rugs. There were two poor reproductions of Van Gogh's landscapes on the wall and a few tattered paperbacks huddled together on a shelf. A TV set, a half-empty bottle of scotch and on the overmantel, a French doll with fuzz glued to her crotch. The trappings of a home, but not much of a home.

But the centre-piece of this sad, sordid room, held me.

Jesse Gordy sat facing me. His hands on the arms of the shabby chair. The front of his blue shirt and his shabby grey jacket were red with blood. At his feet was more blood: a small puddle in which one of his shoes rested.

His lips were drawn back, showing his yellow rat-like

teeth in a snarl of hate and fear. His eyes glared at me: dead eyes, but still hating.

Paralysed with horror, I stared at him. Then the sound of the telephone bell made me stiffen. I looked around, my breathing quick and light. The telephone stood on a table by the dead man.

I stood there, listening to the bell until it finally stopped ringing.

Then in a panic, I started to leave. My immediate thought was to get away, but as I reached the front door, my shock began to recede and my mind began to function.

I paused.

Gordy had been murdered. Someone had either shot or stabbed him. Was that someone a man or a woman Gordy had been blackmailing? Was the film still in the house or had this someone taken it? If the police found the film, both Linda and I would have no future as we knew it now.

Shouldn't I search the house and try to find the film? If the film was found, every wife, photographed stealing, would be investigated by the police. She and her husband would be checked to see if she or he could have murdered Gordy.

Standing there, my mind racing, I suddenly realised that I could be suspect Number one. If questioned, Creeden would say he had met me going toward Gordy's house. I had the motive.

Creeden?

I thought of him as he had come down East Avenue, his spaniel at his heels. He could have killed Gordy. Yes, he fitted. He was big business and ruthless in spite of his ambassador's smile. Rather than let his wife be prosecuted for theft he would have thought nothing of killing a creep like Gordy.

Dare I stay and search the house? Suppose someone came and caught me? The film could be anywhere: cunningly hidden. It could take me hours to search the house.

As I started for the front door, I again paused.

Gordy had been expecting me. Wouldn't he have the snippet of film ready? Why should I care about the rest of the film? It was worth the risk to see if I could find the bit of film that involved Linda, but as I forced myself to turn back to the living-room, I heard a car pull up outside the house.

I whirled around and dashed up the stairs, reaching the upper landing as the front door bell rang. I leaned against the banister rail, looking down into the half lit lobby, my heart hammering.

The bells chimed, then I hear the door push open.

"Jesse?" A woman's voice.

I peered over the rail and caught a glimpse of a woman who moved so swiftly into the living-room I only got an impression of her: small, dark, wearing something dark. I heard her catch her breath, then her scream set my teeth on edge.

"Jesse!"

Slowly, silently, I began to descend the stairs.

"God!"

I heard her dialing. She could only be calling the police. I was now in the lobby.

"It's murder!" Her voice was shrill and hysterical. "Send someone!"

I reached the door, moved silently into the warm darkness. I heard her screaming, "189, East Avenue! It's murder!"

I was ready to run, but instinct warned me. I paused long enough to whip out my handkerchief and wipe the front door handle, the only thing I had touched in the house, then I moved down the path and once on the road, I began to run.

I reached my house, breathless. I had met no one. It was television peak time and everyone, unless throwing a party, was indoors.

With a shaky hand, I got out my front door key and sank it into the lock. It wouldn't turn. I tried again, then pulling out the key, I turned the door handle and the door opened. It passed through my mind, as I entered the dark lobby, that I had forgotten to lock up.

As I closed the front door, I heard the sound of a police siren and saw the lights of a patrol car through the window, storming past and towards East Avenue.

four

IN THE familiar background of my big living-room, I was able to think. I sat in an armchair and considered the situation.

Gordy had been murdered. A woman (who?) had alerted the police who were already on the scene. Before very long more police and the Homicide squad would arrive. They would search the house, hunt for fingerprints and ask around. If they found the blackmail film then Linda and I, Mark and Mabel Creeden, Frank and Sally Latimer and possibly others living on the estate would be on the hot seat. From the film the police would know our wives were thieves: a motive for murder. We all would be checked. If it was discovered that Creeden had been near Gordy's house around the time of the killing, he would be an immediate suspect and as he had seen me, I would also be a suspect . . . unless Creeden kept his mouth shut and I also kept my mouth shut.

It seemed to me my first move was to try to shut Creeden's mouth.

Time was pressing. I went over to the telephone and called his number. His butler answered. I told him who I was and said I wanted to speak to Mr. Creeden. There was a delay, then Creeden came on the line.

"Yes, Steve?"

"Listen carefully, Creeden," I said. "I have information that your wife has been stealing from the Welcome store. My wife has been doing the same thing. I am being blackmailed. I suspect you are too. I went tonight to pay Gordy off. I found him murdered. I saw you in East Avenue where his house is and you saw me. There will be an investigation. I suggest we didn't see each other tonight."

A long pause, then he said, "That makes remarkable sense to me. You didn't see me ... I didn't see you ... right?"

"Yes."

"That's how it will be," he said and hung up.

I put down the receiver and drew in a long breath. It was hard to believe it could be this easy.

Now Linda.

This was something I couldn't do over the telephone. I had to see her. I didn't want to, but I had to. As I got to my feet, I saw the gun and the holster lying on the settee. I picked them up and put them in my desk drawer. Then turning off the light, I left the house, locked the front door and started down the drive. As I reached the gate, I heard a police siren. I watched two police cars sweep past, heading for East Avenue.

I started the long walk to Lucilla's bungalow. Again I heard approaching police sirens and I stepped off the road as another police car, followed by an ambulance went by.

By now my heart was thumping. Fortunately there must have been a good TV show on and the sound had drowned the sirens, otherwise everyone would have been at their garden gates.

I finally reached Lucilla's place, walked up the path and rang the bell.

There was an irritating delay, then Lucilla opened the door.

"Ah, Steve," she drawled. "So you've come to give us good news ... or have you?"

"No good news."

I followed her into the living-room. Linda was still reclining on the settee. She looked at me, her one eye cold and hostile.

"Well?"

Lucilla moved back.

"I'll leave you two dears to talk," she said.

58

"I'd rather you stay. You could be involved in this," I said.

"Really?" She walked over to a chair, sat down and began to fit a cigarette into a foot long holder.

Briefly, I told them that I had gone to Gordy's place, found him murdered and the police were already arriving.

"If Gordy kept the film in the house and the negatives of the blow-ups and the police find them, we are in real trouble." I was talking to Linda. Her face slowly went to pieces and her complexion turned the colour of putty.

"Well, at least you don't have to pay the beastly man," Lucilla said.

Suddenly Linda exploded in hysterical rage.

"I wish to God I had never married you!" she screamed at me. She turned to Lucilla. "Lucy! Help me! What are we going to do?"

Watching her, seeing the way she looked at this middle-aged Lesbian told me Lucilla meant more to her than I ever did.

"Do?" Lucilla tapped ash off her cigarette. "You want a divorce, don't you, my pet?"

"Of course!"

"Well, then, what could be simpler?" Lucilla looked at me. "I imagine you will give Lindy a divorce?"

It came to me what a relief it would be to be rid of Linda. I had had little pleasure from her. For over three years I had put up with her grumbles and her greed.

"Yes."

"Well, then there is no problem. We will leave immediately for Dallas. The story Steve has already put out that your mother has to have an operation is just a cover to stop gossip that you two are divorcing. Don't bother about clothes, Lindy. Steve will send everything you need to Dallas. I'm sure he can give you some money, but if he can't, I can. I'm sure your mother will understand."

Linda began to cry.

"Oh, darling Lucy, I don't know what I would do without you," she mumbled.

Sickened, I took out my billfold and put three thousand dollars I was going to give to Gordy on the table.

"I'll leave you two," I said and started for the door, paused looking at Lucilla. "You really mean you can go tonight?"

She smiled at me.

"I have no problems. You take care of your problems. Within an hour, we'll be on our way."

"The police will check."

"Of course. Men always check, but there will be no problem. You and Linda have been quarrelling. She came to me. I took her to her mother. You wanted to give her money so you told the bank you needed an emergency fund."

I stared at her, then nodded. Then not looking at Linda, I left the room and started the long walk back to my house.

Back home again, I called Jean.

She answered so quickly, I had the impression she had been sitting by the telephone.

"Could we meet somewhere?" I said. "There are complications."

"Come to me? 1190, Westside, top floor."

"In twenty minutes."

As I started to the door, the telephone bell rang. I hesitated, then lifted the receiver.

"Steve? This is Max," Berry said. "I've got the photocopy of the Hammond estimates. It's taken me until now. Man! Will this cut this punk down to size! I've also got photocopies of the three estimates from the other contractors. They really kick the floor under Hammond."

"Wonderful! Let's go over them tomorrow. I have your gun and pistol permit."

He laughed.

"See you tomorrow, Steve. I thought I had to tell you. Linda okay?"

"Sure . . . great work, Max," and I hung up.

Again as I started for the door, I paused. Why go without the gun? I had asked for a gun and I had got it. I would look a pea-brain if I ran into trouble and had left the gun at home.

Taking the gun and the holster from my desk drawer, I put the gun on the desk while I strapped on the holster.

As I was about to put the gun into the holster, I smelt gun powder. I have a very sensitive nose. I can smell things that few people seem able to smell. I lifted the gun barrel to my nose. It had been fired very recently. I stared at it for a long moment, then slid out the magazine. I had loaded the gun with six slugs. Examining the magazine, I found there were only five slugs.

I stood there, feeling a cold chill run through me. The gun had been fired. Was the ejected cartridge case lying on the floor of Gordy's shabby living-room?

*　　*　　*

Jean opened the door of her apartment a moment after I had pressed the bell.

She was wearing a claret-coloured pyjama suit and her feet in embroidered slippers. To me, she looked lovely.

I moved into the big, furnished room as she stood aside.

"More trouble, Steve?" she said as she closed the door.

"I'll say." I looked at her. "I shouldn't have come here, but I just had to talk to someone and who better than you?"

"Sit down and tell me."

"Jean . . . Linda wants a divorce. Our marriage is washed up."

"I'm sorry, but sit down." She moved away from me and sat in a chair a yard or so from the chair she waved to. "Is that the jam or is there more?"

I sat down and told her the whole story of what had happened this evening and concluded with the gun.

"I'm almost certain that someone took the gun, killed Gordy with it and put it back," I said. "So you see . . . I'm really in a hell of a jam."

"But you don't know Gordy was shot. He could have been stabbed."

"The gun was fired. Gordy is dead. Why else was the gun fired?"

She nodded.

"Yes. Let's accept the fact that he was killed with your gun." Her calm, quiet voice had a soothing effect on my jumping nerves. "Let's take a look at this from what we already know. From Wally's report, we can suspect both Latimer and Creeden: both have motives for getting rid of Gordy. You found Latimer outside your house. You tell me the front door was unlocked. Suppose he entered, looking for you, saw the gun and took it? Suppose he went to Gordy's place, killed him while you were talking to Linda, returned and replaced the gun. Creeden could have done exatcly the same thing, couldn't he?"

"Yes, but will the police believe it?"

She sat motionless, her hands gripped between her knees, then she said, "You must get rid of the gun and you must report to the police that it has been lost." She shook her head. "No . . . stolen from your car."

This I hadn't thought of.

"You have the gun with you?" she asked.

"Yes."

"How will you get rid of it?"

How the hell do you get rid of a gun and be sure it wouldn't be found? I thought of the artificial lake on the estate, but could imagine the police would also think of that.

"Dump it in a trash bin down town," I said finally.

"Yes. Give it to me. I'll do it. You must go home, Steve."

"To hell with that for an idea! I'm not involving you!"

"But it will be easy for me. You could be seen doing it. Tomorrow, I'll make a parcel of the gun, put it in my shopping bag and drop it in a trash bin on my way to work."

"That's something you are not going to do." I got to my feet. "I shouldn't have come here. I can handle it."

She smiled wearily, then shrugged.

"All right. Men have to be heroes, don't they? I suppose I mustn't persuade you not to be a hero."

Looking at her, I knew I needed her badly and I knew I was in love with her. I unstrapped the holster and put it on the table with the gun.

"I'm no hero, Jean. I want to say something . . ."

"Please not!" Her voice was curt. "Not now. I'll get rid of the gun. Now go home."

She got to her feet and went to the front door, opening it. I hesitated, then moved by her.

"Thanks," I said. "When this mess has been sorted out, I want badly to talk to you about yourself and myself."

"One thing at a time, Steve," she said quietly and closed the door on me.

I took the elevator down to the lobby and reached my car. I got in and sat thinking.

I wanted so badly to tell her I was in love with her, but she was right, of course. This wasn't the time. I turned my thoughts to my next move. I decided it would be unwise to go to the police and report the gun missing right now. This would have to be done in the morning. My story would be I had left the gun in my glove compartment when I had left the office. I had parked the car the following morning, then remembering the gun, I had found it missing. I had at once driven to police headquarters to report the theft.

So long as Creeden kept his mouth shut, so long as the film showing Linda was a thief wasn't found, then I felt confident, even if the gun was eventually found and proved to be the gun that had killed Gordy, no jury could find me guilty of his murder on such flimsy evidence.

But it didn't work out quite that easily.

As I pulled up outside my garage door, I saw a police car parked across the way. The sight of it set my heart thumping. I got out to open the garage doors as a broad-shouldered, heavily-built man got out of the police car. It was Sergeant Lu Brenner.

"Mr. Manson?"

I turned.

"Hello, Sergeant."

"A word with you."

"Sure. Let me put the car away and come on in."

He stood back. I drove the car into the garage, turned off the lights, then walked around to the front door. By this time I had my jumping nerves under control.

Together we walked into the living-room and I switched on the lights.

"Sit down, Sergeant. What is it?"

I moved to my desk and sat behind it while he stood before me. His craggy face could have been carved from teak. His small, restless eyes kept shifting from me to around the room and back to me again.

"You have a .38 automatic, number 4553 with a pistol permit number 75560?" he asked, staring at me.

"I have an automatic, Sergeant," I said. "I wouldn't know about the number." I took out my billfold and found the pistol permit which I offered him. He examined it, then dropped in on my desk.

"Where's the gun?"

"In the glove compartment of my car."

"I want to see it."

"Why?"

"Never mind why. Go get it."

We stared at each other.

"Have you a search warrant, Sergeant?" I said.

He nodded as if with approval.

"No, but I could get one."

"Suppose you tell me what all this is about. I could then be co-operative, but I'm not just accepting loud talk from you, Sergeant."

He studied me, his little eyes like chips of ice, then he took from his jacket pocket a small object which he set on the desk in front of me. It was a cartridge case.

Keeping my face expressionless, I said, "So?"

"Ever heard of Jess Gordy?"

"He's the manager of the Welcome store up the road." Brenner nodded.

"Yeah. Someone put a slug in him and that's the empty shell I found in the room where he died."

I picked up the cartridge case and rolled it between my fingers. I was expecting him to snatch it away, but he made no move. I looked at him. His expression was blank.

"Isn't this called evidence?" I said.

"Yeah."

I took out my handkerchief and carefully wiped the shell case, then holding it in my handkerchief I set it on my desk.

"You will want it back."

"You keep it. It's a present." He paused, then went on. "Gordy is better out of the way." His rat trap of a mouth curled into a grim smile. "If you haven't already done it get rid of your gun and report it stolen. By shooting that creep you have got a lot of guys off a hook."

"What makes you think I shot him, Sergeant?"

"That cartridge case. It's a new issue. You got the first box. I have to keep track of minor things like that."

"That still doesn't mean I shot him."

"Tell that to the judge." He started towards the door, paused, then said, "Watch it. Lieutenant Goldstein is handling the case. He's up there now, shooting off with his mouth. He could get around to you. I happened to have caught the squeal and I was the first to arrive. He likes me like you like cancer."

"I didn't kill him."

"So long as you can prove it to Goldstein, you didn't kill him."

As he again started to the door, I said, "Sergeant . . ."

He paused to stare at me.

"You made a statement. I'll quote you: 'By shooting that creep you've got a lot of guys off the hook.' Does that include you?"

"Don't get smart, Manson. You could still be in trouble," and he left me.

I sat there, staring at the shell case until I heard his car drive away, then I put the shell case in my pocket.

I remembered Webber had told me Brenner was crazy about his wife. Had she too been stealing from the Welcome store and had Gordy been blackmailing Brenner?

I thought of Lieutenant Abe Goldstein. He was an ambitious, clever cop. If he found the blackmail film, then I would be in real trouble, but so too could Creeden, Latimer and maybe Brenner.

Because I wanted to hear the sound of her voice, I called Jean. There was no answer. I went down to the boiler room and dropped the shell case into the furnace, then I returned to the living-room. I called her number again. Still no answer. I smoked, thought and worried. Half an hour later, I called again.

"Yes."

The sound of her voice was to me like a shot in the arm.

"I've been trying to get you, Jean. I . . ."

"Not now. Tomorrow at the office." Her voice sounded strained. "It's all right . . . you know what I mean. I've just been out. It's all right," and she hung up.

I drew in a long, deep breath. She had got rid of the gun!

I stared into space, thinking.

Another long, lonely night stretched ahead of me.

*　　　*　　　*

I had just finished drinking coffee when I saw the news-boy on his bicycle toss the *California Times* on my stoop. I collected the paper and had to hunt for the account of Gordy's murder. I found it tucked away on page 3.

It merely stated that the manager of the Welcome Self-service had been found by his close friend, Miss Freda Hawes, shot to death. Lieutenant Abe Goldstein was in charge of the investigation. He said the shooting had taken place between 20.30 and 21.00 and appeared to be without a motive.

Obviously the *California Times* was little interested in the murder of Jesse Gordy.

Freda Hawes? A close friend?

How close and did she know Gordy was a blackmailer?

I looked at my watch. The time was 08.15. Time for me to get down to the police and report the loss of my gun. I paused long enough to go through, in my mind, the story I was to tell the police, then locking up, I got the car from the garage and drove into the city. I stopped on the way to buy cigarettes. I always got my cigarettes from the news-stand at the Imperial hotel as there was no parking problem. I was able to leave the car in the forecourt, go into the hotel, get my cigarettes without worrying about a ticket.

The fat good-natured woman who was in charge of the news-stand produced three packs of Winston as soon as she saw me.

"'Morning, Mr. Manson," she said. "I see you have some excitement up at Eastlake."

"That's right." I paid for the cigarettes. "This is a world of violence."

"You can say that again." She shook her head. "Are you going to write about this murder in your magazine?"

"I don't think so. There doesn't seem much information as yet."

"The afternoon editions will have something more. I like an interesting murder case."

In case the police checked my movements, I deliberately stood chatting to her, then abruptly broke off.

"Hey! I have work to do. We've been yakking for ten minutes!"

"So we have." She laughed. "See you, Mr. Manson."

I drove down to my office block.

Joey Small, the night man, was just leaving. Seeing me, he came over.

"'Morning, Mr. Manson. See you have trouble up at Eastlake."

"Yes." I reached over the seat for my brief-case.

"Always trouble for someone these days."

"That's right."

He yawned.

"Will you be working late tonight, Mr. Manson?"

"Could do."

"I'll be seeing you then," and he walked away.

I watched him out of sight, then I backed out of the parking bay and drove down to police headquarters.

The desk sergeant, Jack Franklin, was making motions with a yellow form and looking bored. He was a thickset, middle-aged man who, before his promotion and when he had been a traffic cop, had tried to nail me for dangerous driving. The charge had been thrown out and he had been reprimanded. He was no friend of mine.

When he saw me, his face hardened.

"'Morning, Sergeant," I said, coming to rest at his desk.

"You want something?"

"I'm reporting a gun stolen." I took out my pistol permit and gave it to him. Pushing the end of a pencil into his left ear and twiddling it, he examined the permit, then looked at me.

"So?"

"I put the gun in my glove compartment when I left for home last night. I got to my office this morning, opened the glove compartment . . . no gun."

He took the pencil from his ear, examined it, flicked off a little wax and drew a form towards him.

"Name and address?"

As soon as I said Eastlake, he stiffened.

"You live at Eastlake?"

"That's what I'm telling you."

"You're reporting the loss of a .38 automatic?"

"That's correct."

He pointed a thick finger at a bench against the far wall.

"Sit over there."

"I'm busy," I said. "I'm reporting the gun as stolen. That's all I need do, isn't it?"

"You think so?" He snorted. "Sit over there!"

I didn't move. After glaring at me, he flicked down a switch on his intercom.

"Lieutenant? I have a man here who lives at Eastlake, reporting a .38 automatic stolen."

A mild voice said, "Send him up please, Sergeant."

Franklin pointed to a door.

"First floor: second door."

I walked up concrete steps to a door. I knocked, turned the handle and walked in.

Lieutenant Abe Goldstein sat behind a small shabby desk in a small, shabbier room.

From time to time Linda and I had run into him at the Country club. He was one of the top-class bridge players there. He was a bachelor, and it was whispered that he was a queer, but those who knew him well said he had only two interests; police work and bridge. He was a man a little over forty years of age with steely grey eyes, a big, hooked nose and jet black hair, cut short. He had earned a reputation of being a shrewd, clever police officer without whom Chief of Police Schultz would have long been retired.

"Hello, Mr. Manson," he said. "Is it you reporting a gun lost?"

"Hello, Lieutenant." I advanced to his desk as he stood up. He waved me to a chair. We settled ourselves.

"How is Mrs. Manson?"

"She's okay. Look, Lieutenant, I should be at my desk right now so can we make this fast? I'm reporting the loss of a gun." I gave him my pistol permit. While he was looking at it, I went on, "After Mitford had been attacked, Mr. Chandler thought I should carry a gun. It was delivered yesterday evening. When I left for home, I put the gun in the glove compartment of my car. I thought nothing more of it. Reaching my office this morning, I found it gone."

He pulled a scratch pad towards him and picked up a pen. "Could we get this straight, Mr. Manson? What time did you leave your office last night?"

"Around 19.30."

"You drove straight home?"

"No. I went to the Eat's bar across the street for a quick supper, then I drove home."

"Don't you usually go home for supper?" He looked up, his pen hovering.

"Yes, but last night my wife was with a friend."

"Your car was locked?"

"It wasn't. It was careless of me. I put the gun in the glove compartment, then walked over to the bar. I wanted to get home fast as I had work to do."

"After the meal, you drove straight home?"

"That's right. I picked up some mail and drove over to Miss Bower's place where my wife was. I gave my wife her mail and talked. She and Miss Bower were driving to Dallas because my wife's mother is unwell. I then returned home."

"You left your car outside Miss Bower's place?"

"Yes."

"Unlocked?"

"Yes."

"You got home at what time?"

"Just before nine, I think. I put the car in the garage,

and then settled to work. This morning I drove to the Imperial hotel to get cigarettes. I left my car . . ."

"Unlocked?" Goldstein broke in.

"Yes. I arrived at my office, found the gun missing . . . so here I am.".

Goldstein examined his notes.

"So from the moment you put the gun in your glove compartment you left the car unlocked?"

"Yes. Stupid of me, Lieutenant, but I have lots of things on my mind and locking a car isn't one of them."

He nodded.

"I can understand that. Your magazine is quite something. Well, let's just look at it. While you were having supper, the gun could have been stolen. While you were talking to your wife at Miss Bower's place, it could have been stolen. While you were buying cigarettes at the Imperial hotel, it could have been stolen." He looked up. "Am I right?"

"Yes."

He sat back.

"Stolen guns cause trouble for us, Mr. Manson." He tapped his pen on his thumb nail, then said, "I'm investigating a murder: Jesse Gordy, a neighbour of yours. He was shot with a .38 automatic." His steely grey eyes suddenly stared at me, but I knew this was coming and I kept my expression only half interest.

"I saw it in today's paper. I see what you mean about missing guns causing trouble," I said. "I'm sorry to have been so careless."

"How well did you know Gordy?"

It was my turn to stare at him.

"Is that the drift, Lieutenant? You think the stolen gun killed this man?"

He smiled.

"First, I have to be sure the gun has been stolen, then I'll have to be sure the gun killed Gordy. You haven't answered my question which was how well did you know Gordy?"

"Not at all. I never went to the store. Oddly enough,

70

he came to see me two days ago. This was the first time I had set eyes on him."

Goldstein inclined his head, his thin lips pursing.

"He came to your home?"

"He came to my office. He was interested to know about our advertising rates and whether I could send one of my reporters to write up his store. I explained we didn't take that kind of advertising nor would we be interested in writing up his store."

"He called on you?"

"Yes."

"Couldn't he have telephoned? It's quite a trip from his store to your office."

"I do it every day and think nothing of it."

"Yes." A long pause, then he said, "I am investigating a murder. Since you are here and since you own—or owned, I should say—a .38 automatic, could you tell me what you were doing between 20.00 and 21.00 last night."

I was aware my hands were damp now, but I still kept a deadpan expression.

"I thought I made that clear. I was talking to my wife at Miss Bower's home around 20.15. I returned to my home around 21.00 and I worked until 23.30, then I went to bed."

"Apart from seeing your wife, did you meet any of your neighbours?"

"A little after 20.00 as I was leaving for home I ran into Harry Mitchell whom you know. We talked for a few minutes. After I left my wife, I met Frank Latimer whom you also know and had a word with him. That would be around 21.00."

"No one else?"

Here was the crunch. If Creeden had told Goldstein or would tell him we had met on East Avenue I would be in trouble.

"No one else."

Goldstein put down his pen.

"Thank you, Mr. Manson." As I began to get up, he raised his hand. "May I take up a little more of your time? I have a lot of respect for your magazine and that means respect for your brains. This is an odd murder. Gordy wasn't anything special. I am asking myself why someone should walk into his house and kill him. On the face of it, there appears to be no motive." He stared at me. "You see my problem? Why should anyone want to kill this man?"

"I have no idea." I got to my feet.

"You talked to Gordy. What kind of man would you say he was?"

I wasn't to be drawn.

"As you said: nothing special."

He stared thoughtfully at me.

"Could you enlarge on that?"

"To me he had no personality. Maybe he was competent in his job. I was busy and his proposition didn't interest me so he didn't interest me."

"I understand." He paused, then went on, "His hobby seemed to be photography. He had a well-equipped dark room and a sophisticated enlarger. What surprises me is this, Mr. Manson: although he had this equipment there were no specimens of his work in the house. You follow me?" He rubbed his hooked nose. "Here was a man with an obvious hobby and one would expect to find some photographs, wouldn't you?"

"Seems odd." I shrugged. "The explanation could be he had just started and he hadn't taken any photographs?"

He shook his head.

"No. The developing tank and the fixing dishes had been used. The killer could have taken all the photographs. If he did that, it would give me a motive: that Gordy was a blackmailer."

"Yes. Well, Lieutenant, I have to get to my office."

"Of course." Again he stared at me. "I may have to bother you again, Mr. Manson."

"Sure," I said and left him.

In my car, I sat for some moments while I thought about our conversation. It seemed certain that whoever had shot Gordy had taken the film and the blow-ups. It bothered me that Goldstein had so quickly arrived at a blackmail motive. My big lie was saying I hadn't met Creeden on East Avenue, but Creeden was also involved and I felt sure he wouldn't talk. Then I remembered something else. I had told Goldstein that Gordy had come to my office to talk about advertising. I remembered the tape of his blackmail threat was still on my recorder at home. If Goldstein suddenly descended on me with a search warrant that tape would sink me. I had to wipe it clean and at once. I drove back home. Pulling up outside my house I walked swiftly up the drive, unlocked the front door, entered my living-room and crossed over to where I kept the recorder. I was halfway across the room when I saw the reel of tape was gone. Then I saw something glittering in the sunshine on the floor by the french windows: a small puddle of broken glass. I examined the window. By the lock, someone had smashed a pane of glass.

I went back to the recorder. Whoever had taken the reel of tape had just lifted it and ripped the tape free. A small bit of tape still remained on the tape-up reel. A hurried, panicky job, but whoever had taken the reel now had evidence that Gordy was trying to blackmail me.

The police? I was sure not. The police wouldn't have broken in like this. Then . . . who?

I stood there, controlling a rising panic, knowing the tape could be as damaging as the gun and the film if ever they were found. Then I remembered the blow-up photograph of Linda putting the bottle of perfume in her bag which I had put in my desk drawer. I went to my desk and pulled open the drawer. The blow-up was no longer there.

The sound of the telephone bell startled me.

It was Jean.

"Steve?" Her voice sounded anxious. "What's happening? Are you coming? Your desk is loaded and Max is here, waiting."

Somehow I managed to keep my voice steady.

"I'm on my way," and I hung up.

I took out my handkerchief and wiped off my face and hands. The thought of coping with the business of the office made me cringe, but it had to be done.

Then the front door bell rang.

Looking out of the window, I saw Creeden's Rolls parked at the gate. I went to the front door and opened it.

"I was hoping to catch you," Creeden said. "Just a moment, huh?"

I stood back and let him in.

He moved into the living-room, paused and stared at the broken glass, then he looked at me.

"You've had a break in here?"

"Let's skip that," I said. "Your wife and my wife are thieves. The only way you and I can keep them in the clear and keep ourselves from a murder rap is to keep our mouths shut. I've already been investigated by Goldstein. It'll be your turn before long. I said I didn't see you on East Avenue: you say the same thing."

"You've already talked to the police?"

"Yes. Now, you keep your mouth shut."

"Of course." He moved around the room. "God knows why women have to steal. It isn't as if I keep Mabel short."

"Was Gordy blackmailing you?"

As he said nothing, I went on, "He wanted twenty thousand from me. How much from you?"

He lifted his heavy shoulders.

"Eighty thousand."

"What was his approach?"

"He stopped me in the street."

"He didn't come to your home or office?"

"No. I was getting into my car and he arrived and put on the bite."

"Were you going to pay him last night?"

"Tonight. I had to sell stock."

We looked at each other.

"You realise, don't you, you and I could be suspects for his murder?"

"Yes."

"Well, that's the situation," I said. "You cover for me and I cover for you . . . right?"

74

He stared at me.

"I've never owned a gun." He started for the door, paused and asked, "Have you?"

I met his stare and said nothing.

"I think you could be in a hotter seat than I am," he said, then moving heavily, he left the house and walked down the drive to his Rolls.

five

JEAN HADN'T exaggerated when she had said my desk was loaded. I also found Max Berry pacing around my office like a caged tiger. We spent the entire morning working on the Hammond article. I had no chance to speak to Jean while Max was with me.

Finally, I got rid of him, then Jeremy Rafferty arrived with his piece about violence in the streets. It was so good, I decided to run it in the next issue. I called the artist who did our illustrations and explained to him how to illustrate the article. In spite of being caught up in the machinery of producing a magazine, every now and then my mind kept darting to the stolen reel of tape. When Rafferty left I went into Jean's office but found her in a huddle with one of our advertisers and they looked set for some time. By now it was midday. I asked Judy to phone the Eat's bar and have a sandwich sent over. While I was eating it, I called the hospital to inquire after Wally. I was lucky to catch Stanstead.

"What's the news, Henry? How's Wally?"

"Not so good," Stanstead told me. "He's not responding as he should. I have got Carson coming to look at him this afternoon. Those kicks in the head have done more damage than I had thought."

I stiffened, shocked.

"For God's sake, Henry! You said he wasn't in danger ... is he?"

"Let us say he isn't responding. Carson has seen the X rays. He's deciding whether to operate or not."

"Have you told Shirley?"

"Of course."

"Is he consious?"

"No. You see, Steve, Wally is badly out of condition. He's too fat and bluntly, he's flabby. You can't take the kind of beating he had without being in trouble."

"Who is Carson anyway?"

"He is our best brain surgeon." Stanstead sounded a little impatient that I didn't know. "Mr. Chandler said Wally was to have the best treatment and he's getting it."

"When will you know?"

"Around five o'clock. I'll call you."

"Thanks," and I hung up.

I sat back. I had a definite feeling that Wally could give me information about Gordy. I wanted to know how he had got those three names—Lucilla Bower, Creeden and Latimer and if there were any other names.

The door opened and Jean came in.

"What a morning!" she said. "I have only a minute but I wanted you to know I got rid of the gun last night. I drove down town and dumped it in a sack of refuse. It was the best I could do, but I'm sure it won't be found."

"You are wonderful, Jean. I can't thank you enough. Wally ..."

"I know. I called Shirley. She told me."

"How is she?"

"Bearing up. She's gone to the hospital."

"Stanstead will call me around five."

We looked at each other.

"Will you have dinner with me tonight, Jean? There's a lot to talk about."

The telephone bell started up. She answered, then handed me the receiver. "It's Borg. I'll get back to my desk."

"Tonight?"

"Yes, all right," and she was gone.

"Steve? I hear you've lost your gun." Borg's voice sounded tough.

"It was stolen from my car."

"Hell! I can't get you another and you'd better not

tell the boss. What's the matter with you? Don't you lock your car for God's sake?"

"Last night I had things on my mind."

"Send the permit back to me and I'll try to sort it out. The cops are cursing me," and he hung up.

I remembered that Max and I had been so busy with the Hammond article, I had forgotten to give him his gun and permit. I went over to the closet to check if the gun was still there: it was.

Then Harry Lancing arrived. He handled our financial column which was a big success. He and I spent the rest of the afternoon, interrupted by telephone calls, mapping out his article for the next issue.

When he had gone, the time was nearly 18.00. My intercom buzzed.

"Mr. Chandler on the line," Jean told me.

I lifted the receiver.

"Hi, Steve! I'm just back." Chandler's voice boomed. "Damn good trip. I have things to talk to you about. Come over and have dinner with us and bring Linda. She can keep Lois company while we talk, huh?"

I thought of my date with Jean, but this was an invitation I couldn't refuse.

"Linda is in Dallas with her mother, Mr. Chandler."

"Then bring Jean with you. I have to keep Lois occupied." He laughed. "The Hammond article ready?"

"The layout is with the printers. On my way over to you, I'll get some pulls."

"Fine. Say around seven? I want an early night."

"Yes, Mr. Chandler."

I went into Jean's office and told her Chandler had invited her to dinner.

She threw up her hands, her face registering despair.

"Oh, no!"

"There it is."

"I must drop everything and go home, Steve. I have to change. His wife is so formal. I'll meet you there at seven."

Returning to my desk, I called the printers and asked if they could have pulls of the Hammond article in an hour.

Because Chandler owned the works, they said they would.

I looked at my watch. I had three-quarters of an hour before I need leave the office. In the bustle, I had forgotten Stanstead hadn't telephoned.

I called the hospital. Stanstead apologised for not calling me.

"He's been operated on. I would have called you sooner but Mr. Borg has been taking up my time."

"Borg?"

"That's right. He represents Mr. Chandler, doesn't he? Wally will be all right. In a couple of days, now the pressure on the brain has been removed, he'll be able to have visitors. Mr. Borg wants to get him to some clinic in Miami as soon as it is safe for him to travel. Mr. Chandler certainly looks after his staff."

"In a couple of days, I can talk to him?"

"I think so. The police have priority. Lieutenant Goldstein is already pressing."

"I'll call you Friday."

"Do that."

I sat for a long moment, thinking. Would Wally give the police the story about Gordy? I was sure Shirley would be the first to see him and she must be told to warn Wally to say nothing. I telephoned Wally's house but got no reply. Shirley was probably still at the hospital. Well, I had two days. It was time I was moving. I locked up the office and went down to my car.

I stopped off at the printers and collected the damp pulls of the Hammond article. I paused to look them over. They looked good to me. Then I drove uptown to Chandler's opulent house, arriving there at 19.05. I saw Jean's Porsche already parked. The butler, imported from England, took me into a vast lounge: every piece of furniture had a history and a price, and the paintings in the gilt frames, lit by special lighting, were all museum treasures.

"Come on in, Steve," Chandler said.

Jean, looking lovely in a simple white dress, was nursing a dry martini. Lois Chandler was sitting by her side and she smiled at me as I came forward.

Lois Chandler was some twenty years younger than her husband and that would make her thirty-six or -seven. She was tall, elegant and sophisticated. She appeared to have nothing else to do except entertain her husband's guests, buy clothes, visit beauty parlours and look glamorous. She was so immaculate that I had the feeling that if I touched her it would be like touching a masterpiece in oils that had not completely dried. Her hair, thick and impressively groomed, was tinted sable. Her large green eyes, her rather sharp little nose, her sensual mouth and her determined chin explained why Chandler had married her and doted on her.

"You are a stranger, Steve," she said, smiling at me. "We don't see you enough of you."

We made small talk while drinks were served, then we went into dinner which was formal and over-rich and while we ate Chandler talked about his visit to Washington. We were told how the President was looking, that Chandler thought the inflation problem was on the way to being solved, that the President and he were now on first name terms. While we were being served dessert, Lois suddenly broke in, looking at her husband as she said, "Darling, aren't you monopolising the conversation? I want to hear from Steve about this odd murder at Eastlake."

"You're right, honey." Chandler beamed at her. "Murder? What has happened?"

Lois looked at me.

"You can tell us. Who is this man and why was he shot?"

"I have no idea why he was shot," I said, aware she was staring curiously at me. "He managed the Welcome Self-service store."

"I know *that*! It was in the paper, but why?"

"Even the police don't know. Someone walked into his house and shot him dead. That's all I know." I saw Chandler was looking bored.

"Some drug addict after money," he said impatiently. "It happens every day."

"But surely on the Eastlake estate there are many more

prosperous homes to go to?" Lois said, still looking at me. "I don't suppose this man had much money."

"I wouldn't know."

"Well, I am disappointed," she said and smiled at me. "I was quite, quite sure you would have some inside information. I adore a murder case."

Chandler leaned forward and patted her hand.

"Look, honey, I have to talk to Steve. So suppose you two girls get together, huh?"

Lois lifted her elegant shoulders and turned to Jean.

"Let's go," she said. "Obviously we're outstaying our welcome."

When the door closed behind them, Chandler pushed back his chair and got to his feet.

"We'll go to my study. I want to see the Hammond pulls."

It was not until after midnight that I escaped from his study. By then Jean had gone home and Lois had gone to bed.

Chandler was delighted with the Hammond article. He also talked about the President's anti-inflation plans and together we mapped out an article explaining what the President had in mind. This would have to be written by Lancing. Chandler also talked about the Schultz article. He wanted that to appear in the following issue.

"We'll keep them on the run, Steve," he said, grinning like a schoolboy. "Hit them and keep hitting them. It's good news—Wally will be all right. He's a damn fine researcher. As soon as he's on his feet, I'll send him and his wife down to Palm Beach for some sun. How about a replacement until he can start work again?"

"Berry can handle it. I have a lot of good stuff we haven't used yet."

As he walked me to the front door, he said, "You're doing a fine job. Sorry Linda couldn't come. I like that girl."

I hesitated whether to tell him our marriage had broken down, but decided against it. There was time.

I got in my car, then drove to the Imperial hotel and

using one of the telephone booths, I called Jean. There was a delay, then she answered.

"Could I come over?" I asked. "There's so much to tell you."

"I'm sorry. I'm in bed. I'm utterly exhausted after two hours with that woman. It'll have to wait until tomorrow."

"We never seem to have a moment in the office. Will you have dinner with me tomorrow night so I can bring you up to date?"

"Not tomorrow. I have a date."

"But this is important, Jean. Can't you break it?"

"No."

The curt note in her voice told me that was final. I then began to get worried.

"Jean . . . I know nothing about you. May I ask if there is someone?"

A long pause, then she said, "There is someone . . . yes."

When she said that, I really realised I loved her. I experienced shock and bitter disappointment.

"Really someone?" My voice turned husky.

"I must get some sleep." Again that curt note in her voice told me that too was final. "Good night," and she hung up.

Walking slowly, I went to my car. I had never felt so lonely.

I had known her for eighteen months and had been blind to everything about her except her efficiency. Then suddenly I had seen her as a complete woman. It was like drawing aside a curtain and letting in the sun. I should have known that a girl like her must have a man in her life. Well, I knew now, but it didn't help or console me.

I drove home and put the car in the garage. As I unlocked the door into the house a voice said, "Manson . . ."

I spun around.

Sergeant Brenner was standing in the shadows.

"Turn the light off. I don't want to be seen."

*　　*　　*

83

We sat facing each other in my living-room. As I looked at Brenner I got a shock. This wasn't the hard tough cop that I had known. This was a different man: a man who seemed to have fallen to pieces. His face was white and drawn. The hard lines were ironed out and could there be sudden flabbiness in his body?

"Listen, Manson, I want you to level with me," he said, his big hands turning into fists. "Did you get that film and the blow-ups? Don't lie to me."

"I didn't get them."

He sagged in the chair.

"Goldstein now knows Gordy was a blackmailer. He knows someone has the film."

"If you're in the same mess as I am, suppose we put our cards on the table?"

He regarded me.

"Yeah . . . go ahead. Don't regard me as a cop. Level with me."

"We might help each other," I said. "My wife stole a bottle of expensive perfume from the store. She was caught on the scanner. Gordy wanted twenty thousand dollars for the strip of film, showing her stealing. He told me other husbands were involved. I decided to pay, but I couldn't raise all the money. I went to Gordy's house with three thousand. I found him dead. I was about to search the house for the film when a woman arrived. I got away while she was calling the police. I didn't shoot him, but I'm sure the gun that killed him was the one I was given on the pistol permit. I had left the gun right here on that settee. My thinking is someone took it, killed Gordy, then replaced it. I've got rid of the gun." I stared at him.

"That's the story, Brenner. Feel like giving me your story?"

"The same as yours." He lifted his fists in despair. "Why the hell do women do it? On my pay, I can't give her all that much, but I thought she was happy. The scanner caught her. She was one of the first. The bastard wanted three thousand: that's money I haven't got. So he was selling me a frame from the film at a time for thirty dollars a week."

Although I didn't like him, I felt sorry for him.

"If the film is found," he went on, "I'll be finished. Goldstein has no use for me." He rubbed his hand over his sweating face. "When I got there, I found the shell case. I recognised it and I was sure you had killed him and had got the film and the blow-ups. That was why I gave you the shell case. I knew if Goldstein had found it, he would have traced it to you. My thinking right at that moment was I didn't want anyone nailed for Gordy's murder. That was stupid thinking. Goldstein now knows about the scanners and he has checked the store for film. There's no film. He has checked Gordy's house: no film. So . . . Goldstein is a very smart cookie. He knows Gordy's killing involves blackmail and now he is starting an investigation, checking every customer who has used the store."

"That doesn't mean he can prove anything unless he has the film," I said.

"That's right but he is like a goddamn mongoose. Once he gets his teeth into something, he never lets go."

"Let's look at this Brenner." I was glad to have someone to throw ideas at. "The film and the blow-ups could be in a safe deposit or they could be in the care of someone Gordy trusted or they could have been found by the killer. If they are in a safe deposit, sooner or later, Goldstein will find them. If the killer got them, he will have destroyed them." I paused, then went on, "But if someone Gordy trusted has them, you and I could still be blackmailed."

"I've thought of all that. That's why I was hoping you had them. There's no safe deposit. Goldstein has already checked. This means either the killer found them or else . . ."

"Who is this woman: Freda Hawes?"

"Gordy's mistress. She's a drunken toughie. When I arrived she was slobbering over Gordy, getting herself smeared with his blood, crying and screaming. It was while she was going through her act, I spotted the shell case. God knows if she had seen it. I took a chance."

"Do you know anything about her?"

"I've seen her around. She's a drinker and a hustler. She

hangs around bars, cadging drinks. I don't know anything else about her."

"Maybe it would be an idea to investigate her. I can't do it, but you could." I went on to tell him about Herman Webber and about his story that Gordy's file had been stolen and why I knew he had been lying.

"Webber?" Brenner sneered. "If your boss hadn't set him up as a private eye and financed him, he would be selling matches on the streets. He was going to be booted off the force for corruption, but your boss saved him. That creep would cut his mother's throat for a dollar."

"So he's crooked, but what interests me is why he said the Gordy file had been stolen. What's in the file he doesn't want me to see?"

Brenner nodded.

"Yeah . . . you have something there. Do you think he has destroyed the file?"

I shrugged.

"I don't know. Look, Brenner, I'm not the only suspect around here." I went on to tell him about finding Frank Latimer outside my house and how I had run into Creeden coming away from Gordy's place. "Either of them could have walked into my house, taken the gun and killed Gordy. They had the same motive. Their wives had also been stealing."

"I'll listen around. What I want to be sure of is the film has been destroyed."

"Can you get me some information about Freda Hawes?"

"Sure, but you can bet Goldstein will be onto her by now." He leaned forward and poked a thick finger at me. "I'm working on the inside and you will be working on the outside, together we could find the film before Goldstein does. But listen, Manson, this between you and me and no one else. You talk to anyone and I'll repeat that . . . you talk to anyone including your staff, we could be in trouble. So say nothing. We will work together, but no one else . . . understand?"

I thought of Jean. I had been going to tell her about Brenner. I loved her and I wanted to have her thoughts and advice, but now looking at Brenner's drawn, anxious face, I realised there was no point telling her. She had someone else. I wasn't in her life. I must not involve her.

"I understand."

He got to his feet.

"We mustn't be seen together, Manson. If you get something or I get something, we use the telephone. If we have to meet, I'll come here late, but it is safer not to meet."

He went away, leaving me feeling a little less lonely, but not much.

*   *   *

When Cissy arrived the following morning, I told her I had forgotten my keys and had to. break in and could she get her husband to repair the window. She rolled her eyes and beamed and said it would be fixed by the time I returned.

I then told her that Mrs. Manson had gone to see her mother and would Cissy pack a couple of suitcases with clothes and have them sent to Dallas. I gave her three dollars for her trouble.

Having settled my home worries, I got in the car and drove to the office. I felt a little embarrassed facing Jean but I need not have been. She was her usual quiet, efficient self and we immediately got caught up in the machinery of the magazine. It wasn't until close on midday when she came in with printer's proofs that she said, "I'm sorry about tonight, Steve. Is there anything you want to tell me? We have a few moments."

"I've been thinking about it, Jean." I looked at her. "You have done enough. I could be in a jam but I'm not involving you further. The fact you got rid of the gun is more than enough." I forced a smile. "It'll work out."

"I'm not scared of getting involved. If I can help, I want to help."

"It's okay and thanks for the offer." I paused, then went on, "Whoever it is, Jean, I hope you will be happy."

She flushed a little, then putting the proofs on my desk, she said, "Thank you. I'll go to lunch. I won't be long," and she left me.

I sat for some moments feeling sorry for myself. I wondered who the man was, then the telephone brought me back to work. Later, I remembered I hadn't warned Shirley to tell Wally to keep his mouth shut about the Welcome store.

I called her home.

When she came on the line, I said, "Great news about Wally! You must be relieved."

"Oh, boy! You can say that again." Shirley sounded very elated. "I'm seeing him tomorrow afternoon. I might see him sooner. It depends on what Dr. Stanstead says."

"Shirley . . . I hate to bother you with this, but the police will talk to Wally. It is essential he says nothing about the Welcome store. Would you tell him that?"

"The Welcome store? I don't understand."

"Wally has been researching the store. He's not to tell the police."

"But he hasn't!" A pause, then she said, "Well, at least, he didn't tell me about it."

"I think he has. We are not ready yet to give out publicity to anyone but the store. It's important."

"I'll tell him, of course. Isn't there a murder inquiry going on about the store? I've been so het-up, I have scarcely looked at a newspaper."

"That's right. That's why it's important for Wally to say nothing until I've talked to him. This is really important, Shirley. Mr. Chandler wants it that way."

"All right, Steve. I'll tell him . . . say nothing about the Welcome store . . . right?"

"That's it . . . nothing to nobody. Did Chandler tell you he is sending you and Wally to Palm Beach once Wally is on his feet?"

"He told me. He's a wonderful boss, Steve."

"Yes. I hope to see Wally sometime tomorrow afternoon," and I hung up.

On an impulse, I picked up the telephone book and looked up Freda Hawes. She was in the book: 1189, East Street: not a good district: on the fringe of the city's little Harlem.

I was wondering about her when Max Berry came in and from then on until I had lunch I was occupied.

I went to my club for lunch and as I sat down at a table, Harry Mitchell joined me.

We both had the rather dreary businessman's lunch: mostly lettuce and tomatoes with a thin slice of ham.

We talked of this and that, then Mitchell said, "Steve, you know, in Eastlake, we live in a goldfish bowl. Punch me on the jaw if I'm stepping out of turn, but rumour says you and Linda are parting. Now . . . wait. If I've said anything out of turn, say so and let's forget it, but this happens to be important to me."

I stared at him.

"I'm not with you."

"Could you confirm that you and Linda are parting?" He forked up a bit of tomato, then put it back on his plate.

"I can confirm that."

"I'm sorry, but I can see how it is. Linda needs living with." He grinned at me. "Look, Steve, do you plan to stay on in that big house? If you don't, I have a buyer for you."

I sat back, my lunch forgotten. The idea of being saddled with the house, with Cissy bleeding me white was a sudden nightmare I hadn't thought of.

"I could be in the market," I said cautiously.

He leaned forward and patted my wrist.

"Man! Have I good news for you! Mom and Dad have been dying to live at Eastlake. We all get along fine together. There has been no house vacant I could fix for them. You paid seventy-five thousand dollars . . . right?"

"Yes."

"My old man is loaded. Suppose he offers eight-five? Would you be interested?"

"I'll have to think about that, Harry. Property has jumped way ahead. Give me a week, huh?"

He pushed his salad this way and that, then he said "I've already talked to Dad. He's crazy mad to have your place. Look, he's already got two homes. He doesn't want to bother to refit another house. I know your place. It has class. Would you sell it as it stands: all the furniture, the linen and so on? Would you do that?"

I drew in a long deep breath.

"I might do, but this is a little sudden."

He paused while he chewed some ham.

"Sure. Would a hundred thousand, including the furniture and fittings interest you?"

"For a hundred and thirty thousand, Harry, you have yourself a deal."

He grinned widely and slapped me on the shoulder.

"You old horse thief! It's a deal. Man! How I love spending other people's money! When can they move in?"

"When I get the money, I move out."

"That's fighting talk." He produced a cheque book, scribbled and handed the cheque to me.

"Okay. So I move out at the end of the week."

"This calls for a drink. What will you have?"

I shook my head, pushed back my chair and stood up.

"I have a magazine to produce, Harry. Tell your parents they can move in if they want to next Monday." I patted his shoulder and walked away, leaving most of my lunch uneaten.

* * *

Back in the office, I told Jean about the deal.

"It's fantastic! A hundred and thirty thousand! No bother about getting rid of the funiture and I'll be shot of Eastlake!"

"I'm so glad," she said, "but you will be homeless. You have only five days to move out."

In my excitement to get all that money and to be rid of the house, I hadn't thought of that.

"I'll go to a hotel."

"Do you want to live in the city?"

"I guess so. This commuting has been driving me crazy."

"I'll find you a service apartment. That's no problem. If you will put everything you want to keep in one room, I'll arrange for someone to pack and deliver it to the apartment."

I stared at her. If only she could be my wife!

"That's marvellous, Jean. Will you really do that?"

"Of course. That's what I'm paid for." She smiled to take the curse off that. "I'll fix it," and she left me.

I got away from the office soon after 18.00. As I was walking to my car, Frank Latimer came from his office building.

"Hi, Steve! What's this I hear . . . you leaving Eastlake?"

I knew I was going to get a lot of this so I made it short.

"That's right. Linda and I are parting. I don't want to keep the house."

"I'm sorry." He wagged his head. "When Harry told me, I couldn't believe it. Still, you have done a swell deal with him. His old man must be loaded to turn out that kind of money. We'll miss you. Come on over and have dinner with us."

"I have packing to do . . . thanks all the same."

"Well, because you're leaving Eastlake that doesn't mean we won't see you. Sally will be upset. Like me, she loves you two."

"That's the way the cookie crumbles," I said and got in my car.

How glad I would be to be rid of Eastlake! Every move, every whisper were known in seconds. At least, living in the city I would be out of the goldfish bowl.

I spent a depressing evening and half the night putting my personal things and Linda's things in the study. I was surprised they amounted to so little. Cissy had packed most of Linda's clothes. I had to pack mine. There were books, gramophone discs and a few nicknacks but little else.

Finally, around midnight, I went to bed, but not to sleep.

I kept thinking of that reel of tape that had been stolen. I also kept thinking of Jean. She was really marvellous. All right, she had said that was what she was paid to do, but that didn't make her any less marvellous to me. What really kept me awake until the small hours was the knowledge that Harry Mitchell had yakked around that he was

91

paying me one hundred and thirty thousand dollars for my house. If there was a second blackmailer, and I felt in my bones there was, this news if it reached him/her would be like sweet music. I wondered too if Brenner had found out anything about Freda Hawes. Could she be the second blackmailer if there was to be one?

I thought of tomorrow. With luck I might have a word with Wally. I realised how much I was relying on him to get me clear of this jam. He must have got his information about the stealing from someone, and maybe this someone could point to Gordy's killer and get me off the hook.

Reaching the office the following morning, I told Jean I had put all my personal things in the study and she said she would take care of it. I gave her a duplicate key to the front door.

"I've asked around, Steve," she went on. "There's a good furnished apartment on Eastern Avenue which I think you will like. Would you take a look at it lunchtime?"

"As quick as that?"

She smiled.

"I hope you will like it." She put a slip of paper on my desk. "Here's the address and the rent and the name of the agents. The rent comes a little high, but I think you'll agree it is worth it."

"You have seen it?"

"I looked at it last night."

I regarded her.

"But you said you had a date last night."

"I can do two things at once. I was a little late, but I wanted you to be fixed up." Then picking up the mail and before I could thank her, she went back to her office.

I had a quick lunch then drove to Eastern Avenue: a good district, overlooking the park. The janitor, a large, smiling Negro who told me his name was Sam Washington ("No relation to the great Mr. George, Mr. Manson") showed me the apartment. It couldn't have been better. It consisted of a large bedroom, a large sitting room and the rest, comfortably furnished.

I said I would take it.

"Yeah, Mr. Manson, you could do a lot worse."

I returned to the office, thanked Jean and she said she would fix it with the agents.

Around 17.00 I telephoned the hospital and was again lucky to catch Stanstead.

"Can I see Wally?" I asked.

"Suppose we make it tomorrow morning, Steve? He has already seen his wife and also Lieutenant Goldstein. I think he has had enough for today."

"This is really important, Henry. I promise I won't stay for more than ten minutes."

"Well, all right, if it is that important. No longer than ten minutes."

I told Jean I was seeing Wally.

"I'll get you some flowers and give him my love."

I arrived at the hospital soon after 18.00, carrying a bouquet of violets. I ran into Stanstead who was leaving.

"How is he?" I asked.

"Better than I thought possible, but he still needs care. His eye will be all right. There is also a suggestion of amnesia. The police didn't seem satisfied."

I smiled to myself. Shirley had got the message home.

I took the elevator to the third floor, found Wally's room, tapped and entered.

Wally, his head in bandages, one eye covered, lay in the bed. As I closed the door, I said, "Wally! Is it good to see you!"

"Hello, Steve." His voice sounded depressingly feeble. "Good of you to come."

I put down the violets.

"From Jean . . . she sends her love."

"Great girl." His hands moved over the sheet.

"How do you feel?"

"Not so good."

Looking at him I realised the truth of what Stanstead had said about Wally being too fat and too flabby.

"You're going to be all right, Wally. As soon as you can get on your feet you and Shirley will be off to Palm Beach."

"Yes." He didn't appear to be particularly pleased.

"Wally . . . I musn't stay long. Stanstead said ten

minutes, but this is important. Jean told me you have been researching the Welcome store and you have come up with three names . . . Lucilla Bower, Mabel Creeden and Sally Latimer. Who told you?"

His fat face was as expressionless as a hole in a wall.
"I don't understand."

"Did you research the Welcome store?"

"No."

I began to feel a chilly sensation.

"Think, Wally. How did Jean get those names unless from you?"

"I don't know what you are talking about."

"Wally, please concentrate. This is vitally important to me to know the source of your information. I know you are always secretive about where you get your facts, but this time, because you and I are close friends, I ask you who told you these three women were stealing from the store."

He lay there: a fat, broken lump and stared at me.

"I don't know what you're talking about."

"What did you have in your brief-case that was stolen?"

His one eye closed and he moaned a little.

"The Hammond thing."

"Nothing about the Welcome store?"

"I don't know a thing about that. I don't know even what you are saying."

Leaning forward, my voice hard, I said, "Wally! Pull yourself together! Think! You have been working on this stealing! You found someone who talked. You got names! Wally! Who was this someone?"

Okay, I was getting worked up and I must have raised my voice for the door opened and a nurse came in.

"Your time is up, Mr. Manson," she said in that flat final voice nurses have.

"Wally!"

"I don't know anything," he said and putting his hands to his bandaged head, he began to groan,

The nurse practically threw me out. I walked down the corridor, into the elevator and into the night.

I stood by my car. Wally had been my big hope. I had

a feeling that a door was slowly shutting and I was trying to hold it open, but the force of the door as it closed was pushing me back and defeating me.

Was Wally really suffering from amnesia or had someone so badly frightened him he was lying to me . . . as Webber had lied to me?

Leaving my car, I crossed the road to a drug store and rang Jean. There was a delay, then she answered.

"Jean . . . it's Steve. I've just seen Wally. He says he hasn't researched the Welcome store. Did you keep a copy of his report you typed?"

A pause, then she said, "No."

"But you're sure he did mention Lucilla Bower, Mabel Creeden and Sally Latimer?"

"I am quite sure. I did warn you, Steve, that Wally just won't give his informants away?"

"You said there were other names. Try to think, Jean. It's important."

"I've already thought. I'm sorry, Steve. I can't remember any of the other names. His report was very brief. It said he had evidence that a number of women living at Eastlake had been stealing from the store. He then gave names. This was scribbled in his notebook. I typed it and gave him two copies."

"His notebook?"

"That's right."

"Maybe Shirley would have that."

"Should I ask her?"

"No. I'll do it. Well, thanks Jean . . . see you tomorrow."

I got in my car and drove over to Wally's home.

Shirley welcomed me. After talking about Wally and her delight about going to Palm Beach, I said, "Shirley, Wally had notebooks. I need them. Do you know where they are?"

"Why sure. Mr. Webber took them all when he came. He said Mr. Chandler wanted them. You ask him . . . he'll give them to you."

"Herman Webber?" I stared at her.

"He was here just as I got back. He said Mr. Chandler wanted all Wally's notebooks."

"I see. I'll talk to him."

"You do that." She wrinkled her pretty nose. "I can't say I like Mr. Webber very much."

"Neither do I," I said and left her.

six

HERMAN WEBBER was a big, heavily-built man who looked every inch a cop. His face could have been carved out of granite. His small blue eyes probed. His thin lips remained in a hard, unsmiling line.

"Hello, Steve," he said, not getting up from behind his desk. "Sit down. What's cooking?"

As soon as I had gone through the morning mail and had dictated to Jean, I had dropped everything and had driven over to Webber's office.

"Wally's notebooks," I said, sitting down. "Shirley tells me you have them."

"Yeah."

I stared at him.

"What's the idea?"

"Playing it smart." Webber pulled at his cigar, clenched between his teeth and released a cloud of smoke in my direction. "That's what I'm here for . . . to play it smart."

"So?"

"That punk Goldstein has been questioning Wally. He wants to know who gave Wally the tip-off that Hammond has been padding the accounts. Wally always protects his informants. I know Wally keeps names in his notebooks so before Goldstein could get around to Shirley, I got around and I have the books."

It sounded good, but too smooth to me.

"So Shirley tells Goldstein—as she told me—that you have the books. So Goldstein comes to you and what do you do?"

Webber blew smoke at me.

"Shirley is a co-operative girl. She won't tell Goldstein. Like I said: I've played it smart."

"Fine." I stared at him. "Wally works for me. I want those books."

He nodded.

"If you want them, you can have them." He flicked down a switch on his inter-com. "Mavis? Get me Mitford's notebooks. Put them in a sack. Mr. Manson wants them." He looked at me. "Okay? Well, I guess you have work to do . . . me too."

"The Gordy file," I said. "I want it."

His eyes turned a little sleepy.

"I told you . . . some nut stole it with other files."

"Come on! Don't feed me that crap! I have reason to believe you didn't have a break in. I want that file!"

"Yeah?" He was too much of a cop to betray any feelings. "What are you talking about?"

"I want that file. I believe you have it and I want it."

"I told you, pal, it was stolen. I haven't got it."

"Gordy's been murdered. Do you want me to tell Goldstein you had a break-in and Gordy's file was stolen. I either get the file or that's what I'll tell him."

"Go ahead." Webber tapped ash off his cigar. He looked very sure of himself. "Why should I care?"

"I'll tell you why. Goldstein will want to know why you didn't report the break-in and knowing Gordy has been murdered why you haven't reported the theft of his file. He must love you. He could stick it in and turn it."

"You think so?" He leaned forward, his little eyes suddenly glaring. "And you could land yourself in much more trouble if you start shooting your mouth off to Goldstein!" His cop voice was like a punch in the face. "Keep your snout out of this. I'm telling you!" He waved to the door. "Piss off! I've work to do!"

I got to my feet.

"I'll talk to Mr. Chandler. It's time he knew what's going on."

"Yeah?" He sat back and his thin lips twisted into a

sneering grin. "Take another think. Can't you get it into your skull that I am protecting you? You drag the boss into this and you're really in the crap. Now piss off and let me get on with my work!"

I then realised he had the ace against my queen. *I'm protecting you*. That must mean he knew about Linda and her thieving.

As I went into the outer office, Mavis Sherman, thin, dark and worried looking, handed me a plastic sack stuffed with Wally's notebooks.

Back in my office, I had laid the books on my desk. There were fourteen of them. Each book was numbered from one onwards. I found No. 13 was missing. I didn't bother to examine the books. I was sure No. 13 covered the stealing at the Welcome store. Like the Gordy file, it had gone missing.

I sat back and thought about the situation. Webber's warning told me I couldn't go to Chandler. If I got tough with Webber, he could get tougher with me. I was sure someone (Webber?) had thrown a scare into Wally. Maybe this was wrong thinking. The beating Wally had had could have scared him, but I didn't think so. I felt almost sure that Wally had been warned as I had been warned. Keep your mouth shut or else . . .

I decided I would have to see Wally tonight. Maybe if I confided in him, handling him gently, telling him about the mess Linda had landed me in, I could persuade him to talk.

The telephone bell rang and from then until lunch-time I was caught up in the business of producing a magazine.

After lunch, Jean came in to tell me my personal things had been packed and had been taken to the Eastern Avenue apartment.

"You can move in whenever you like," she said. "It's all ready. I've ordered a stock of groceries: coffee, milk and canned food."

"You're really wonderful, Jean," I said, looking at her with an ache in my heart. "I'd like to buy you a very expensive dinner . . . may I?"

"Thanks, but no."

"This invitation also includes your boy-friend. I would like to meet him."

She regarded me, her eyes serious.

"Look, Steve, please leave me my private life. It's my job to look after you in the office and at home if I can. May we leave it like that?" She gave me a ghost of a smile, then returned to her room.

Well, I thought, that was final enough.

I was kept busy until after 18.00, then I left Jean to lock up and drove to the hospital. I went to the reception desk and ask if I could see Mr. Wally Mitford.

"You've missed him," the girl told me.

I gaped at her.

"Missed him? What do you mean?"

"He left with his wife in an ambulance half an hour ago."

Again I felt that chilly sensation.

"Where has he gone?"

"I don't really know."

"Is Dr. Stanstead still here?"

"He's in his office."

I found Stanstead preparing to go home.

"What's all this about Wally? I'm told he's gone."

He shrugged. He looked weary and harassed.

"I don't approve, but there it is. They've taken him by ambulance to the airport and are flying him to Miami. He wanted to go and he was fit enough to travel . . . so he's gone."

"Was this something Mr. Chandler arranged?"

"I guess so. Mr. Borg handled it."

"Shirley went with him?"

"Yes. He's to go to some clinic either in Miami or Palm Beach."

"You don't know the clinic?"

"No. Look, Steve, I've got more work than I can cope with," he said impatiently. "I'm sure Wally will be in good hands and the sun will do him good."

"Yes. Well, see you, Henry," and I left the hospital, got in my car and sat thinking.

Was there a conspiracy going on? First Gordy's file,

the film and the blow-ups had vanished, then the reel of tape, recording Gordy's blackmail threat to me, had been stolen, then Wally's notebook had gone missing and now Wally had been whisked out of reach. I had an uneasy feeling that someone was breathing down my neck.

What to do?

The door now seemed shut. Trying to control a rising panic, I told myself the only thing I could do was to sit it out and hope nothing would develop. Maybe nothing would, but I felt sure, at the back of my mind, I was kidding myself.

I started to drive home. This was a reflex action. Halfway, I remembered there would be no food in the house so I pulled into the forecourt of the Imperial Hotel. There I had a steak. As I was paying the check, the frontman came over to me.

"Mr. Manson?"

"That's right."

"There's a telephone call for you . . . booth 5."

Surprised, I took the call. It was Sergeant Brenner.

"Saw your car," he said curtly. "I want to talk to you. Do you know the Half Moon bar?"

"I don't."

"It's on 15th Street, next to the drug store. You can't miss it. Take a cab: you can't park anyway. Ask for Jake. See you in half an hour," and he hung up.

I picked up a cab outside the hotel, leaving my car in the hotel's forecourt.

The Half Moon bar was sleazy and half empty. There were three painted hookers propping up the bar. A couple of coloured men were drinking beer at one of the tables. A dirty-looking youth with hair to his shoulders was sitting at another table, aimlessly picking his nose.

As I walked up to the bar, a beefy man in shirt sleeves flopped a dirty rag in front of me and began polishing.

"You Jake?" I asked.

He eyed me over, nodded, then jerked his thumb towards a door. Watched by the three hookers, I pushed open the door, climbed a short flight of stairs and pushed open another door.

Brenner was nursing a beer. The room was small: a bed, a table and two chairs. A torn blind screened the window. I closed the door.

"This looks like a set for a B movie," I said, joining him at the table.

"Yeah, but it's safe. Jake owes me a lot. I could have put him away for five years. Sit down."

I pulled up a chair and sat down."

"Freda Hawes," Brenner said. "I've checked her out and so has Goldstein. She says nothing, even under pressure. She says she slept with Gordy from time to time, but she knows nothing about him. She's scared and she's lying. She's not opening her mouth to the Law, but she just could talk to you. I could be wrong, but it's worth a try."

"She could be a blackmailer. She could have the film and the blow-ups. I don't want to tangle with her."

"I'll be surprised if she is. She's not the type and I know blackmailers. Go take a look at her. She hangs out at the Blue Room on 22nd. You'll find her there any time from now to dawn. She's a drinker. If you think you can handle her, talk to her. When a guy sleeps with a woman, sooner or later, he lets his hair down. I'm pretty sure Gordy has stashed away that film somewhere. He might have told her. That's our only hope, Manson. We've got to get that film before Goldstein does."

I didn't like this, but at least, I could take a look at this woman.

"How do I know her?"

"Short, dark, around twenty-five, well built," Brenner said. "You can't miss her. Her thing is to wear brass bracelets that crawl half way up her arms."

"Okay, I'll take a look." I then told him I was moving into the apartment on Eastern Avenue. He wrote down my telephone number.

"Goldstein has talked to Creeden, to Latimer and the rest of them," Brenner went on. "Kid glove stuff. Very smooth, gentle, just probing, but he's probing. He'll come to you next, so watch it. He is asking have you any idea that there was stealing at the Welcome store? Of course everyone has been open-eyed and saying no, but Goldstein

102

is a damn smart cookie. He digs in the question fast and there is always a blink of the eyes and that is what he is watching for. He's got nowhere so far, but once he gets his teeth into a murder case, he is hard to shake loose."

"I'll watch it." I wondered if I should tell him about the reel of tape and about Wally's notebook. I decided not. I had a feeling that I would be better off if I kept my mouth shut from now on and tried to work this out on my own.

"I'll go along to the Blue Room right away. Suppose you call me tomorrow morning at the office? We could meet here again if I have anything."

"Yeah, but I don't want to call you. Let's meet: this time tomorrow."

"Okay."

I left him, made my way down the stairs, nodded to Jake who nodded back, then went out onto the busy street to find a cab.

*　　*　　*

The Blue Room was a cellar club on the corner of 22nd and East which placed it near Freda Hawes's pad.

The cabbie who drove me there looked searchingly at me as I paid him.

"It's not my business, buddy," he said when he saw the size of my tip, "but that joint is strictly not for you. If you're yearning to get mugged you're heading in the right direction."

"Thanks."

I stepped back. He stared at me again, lifted his heavy shoulders and drove away.

Looking up and down the street, I saw what he meant and I hesitated. I was wearing a business suit and when I saw the kind of flotsam drifting up and down the street I felt as conspicuous as a bishop in a brothel.

While I had served in the army, I had taken a combat course. Not like Wally Mitford, I kept in shape. I was confident I could take care of myself. It would have been better to have gone home and changed into less conspicuous clothes, but now I was here, I was damned if I was going home, to change and come all the way back.

There was a small neon sign that read:

BLUE RO M

The second O was missing.

I went down a long steep stairway, and as I descended, the noise of swing and the smell of unwashed bodies increased until I reached a tiny lobby.

A big Negro sat on a stool, staring into space. He showed only the whites of his eyes. A second look told me he was turned on and wouldn't know if he was on this earth or on the moon.

A red curtain screened the entrance and I lifted it aside and looked in.

The big room was packed with dancing figures and dark enough to make them weaving silhouettes. The noise of the four-piece band exploded against my eardrums. The smell of unwashed feet, dirt and reefers was choking.

To walk into that inferno, dressed as I was, would be to invite suicide. I dropped the curtain, deciding I would go along to Freda Hawes's pad and wait for her there. As I started up the stairs two youths started down.

I stopped and so did they.

In the dim light, I could see they were around twenty years of age. Their filthy hair reached to their shoulders. Their white, dirty faces were pinched and their little eyes had the glitter of junkies.

"Look who's here," the taller of the two said. "A snout poker. What do we do to snout pokers, Randy?"

"Stomp him," Randy said. He was weaving a little: either drunk or drugged. "Let's get him up on the street, Heinie. Don't want to wake up old Sam."

Heinie beckoned to me.

"Come on, creep, unless you want to be cut." A flick knife jumped into his hand.

I started up the stairs and they slowly retreated until

they moved out onto the street. I had three more stairs before I joined them in the open. I jumped those stairs, hit Randy a chopping blow on his neck, weaved around Heinie, grabbed his wrist and heaved him judo-style over my back. He crashed down on the sidewalk.

I walked fast around the corner onto East Street, kept moving and told myself I was crazy to have come to this district dressed the way I was. The encounter with those two junkies showed me the red light. I had to get out of here fast. I looked around for a cab, but cabs kept clear of East Street.

Then out of an alley, three long-haired youths who must have been watching my approach, burst out and grabbed me. I was dragged into the alley, off balance and unprepared.

I went limp. My weight took them by surprise and the two holding me collapsed with me onto the evil-smelling concrete. I threw them off, kicked out at the third figure, silhouetted against the open alley, a bottle raised in his hand. I caught him in the crotch and he went over, screeching. One of the others heaved himself on me and we went down with a thud. I chopped the side of his neck hard and he flattened out. The last one lost his guts and ran.

I leaned against the wall, getting my breath back, then I moved onto the street, stepping over the one I had kicked who was screwed up, holding himself and mewing like a cat. I knew I must be in a mess. My sleeve was torn. I could smell the refuse sticking to the back of my jacket.

Keeping in the shadows, I walked down East Street. I remembered Freda Hawes's number. When I came to her block. I climbed five steps and entered a dimly-lit lobby. The mail box told me she was on the fourth floor. There was no elevator. I climbed, walked down a corridor to a door that read: *Miss Freda Hawes. By appointment. Tel. East 4456.*

I thumbed the bell and waited.

Somewhere on the second floor a woman screamed: "No! I tell you no! Keep away from me!" Then silence. I heard heavy footsteps pound up the stairs, but they stopped on the third floor. Looking over the rail, I saw a thickset man entering one of the apartments.

I thumbed the bell again.

While I waited I took off my jacket and shook off the potato peeling, the dead cabbage leaves and other horrors that had been sticking to me.

It became obvious that Freda Hawes was not at home. This presented a problem. If she was at the Blue Room she could jive until three or four in the morning. I couldn't stay out in this exposed corridor for some six hours. I would also be risking my neck if I appeared on the street. I had to get to a telephone and get a cab to pick me up. Where was the nearest telephone?

I looked at the door and the card. She had a telephone. Maybe the lock was brittle. I turned the handle and was startled when the door swung open.

I paused. The chilly sensation began to crawl up my spine. Was I going to have a repeat performance? Was I going to find Freda Hawes shot to death?

As I stood there, I heard a soft moaning sound that made the hair on the nape of my neck bristle. Then I heard someone coming up the stairs. Hurriedly, I stepped into the dark room and shut the door.

I smell fresh cigar smoke.

A neon sign across the way was flashing on and off, spelling out:

GIRLS! GIRLS! GIRLS!

Its red light kept lighting up the small room. Across the way was a door that stood ajar.

I heard heavy footfalls pass and go on up the stairs. A trickle of sweat ran down my face. My mouth was dry. My heart was thumping.

The moaning sound came from the inner room.

Bracing myself, I fumbled my way over to the door and peered into the darkness. I could make out the outline of a bed, but nothing else. My hand slid down the wall, found a light switch. I hesitated, then turned the switch up.

The harsh overhead light made me blink.

The scene that came into my view made me catch my breath.

A woman, stark naked, lay on the bed. Her wrists were tied to the bedposts, her ankles too. She had a rag stuffed into her mouth. On her right thigh was a livid round burn: a burn that could have only been made by crushing a burning cigar end into her flesh.

I knew this was Freda Hawes. She was small, beautifully built, around twenty-five. A few years back, she could have been pretty, but now the edges had hardened, the mouth, the eyes showed the steady downward slide.

All this I took in in one brief glance, then I reached her, got the gag out of her mouth and her wrists untied. Then I started to free her ankles.

"A drink . . . the kitchen," she croaked.

I found a light switch in the living-room, found the kitchen, opened the refrigerator. It was stocked with bottles of gin and charge water. I found a dirty glass which I rinsed under the tap, poured a heavyweight slug of gin and a featherweight slug of charge water. I hurried back and seeing how her hands were shaking, I lifted her head and fed her the drink.

She drank greedily, shut her eyes, her fingers gripping my wrist.

"More!"

"That'll hold you," I said gently. "You . . ."

"More! Hear me, you sonofabitch! More!" There was a yell of despair in her voice so I went back and produced the mixture as before.

When I returned she was sitting up on the side of the bed, the sheet across her lap. She snatched the glass from me, drank, then threw the glass across the room. It shattered against the wall.

"Cigarette!"

I took out my pack, lit a cigarette and fed it between her trembling lips.

She sat still, her heavy breasts hanging forward, dragging at the cigarette, letting smoke drift down her pinched nostrils. I stood back and watched her.

After some minutes, the gin began to work. She looked up and stared at me.

"Who are you?"

"Just passing. I heard you making noises, so I looked in," I said, sure she wasn't ready yet for me to show my hand.

She nodded.

"I've always been lucky. I thought I was going to stay right there until next month. Sit around. I like you. I want a pee."

She wobbled across to the bathroom and shut herself in. On the floor, by the bed, lay a stub of a cigar. I picked it up and regarded it. It meant nothing to me or was the smell a little familiar? My nose again, I thought and laid the cigar on the night table.

She came out of the bathroom, opened a closet, put on a wrap, then walked into the kitchen. I heard the gurgle from bottles and she came back with another glass in her hand.

"Thanks, boy scout. Keep this close to your chest. I'm fine now. Take the breeze, will you?"

"Lieutenant Goldstein should be told about this," I said gently.

She slopped her drink, then stared at me, her big dark eyes opening wide.

"You're not another of those bastards, are you?"

"Have there been more than one?"

She sat on the bed, motionless for some moments, then she drank half the contents of the glass, shuddered, then looked around as she dropped the cigarette end on the floor. I picked it up and crushed it out in an ashtray, lit another cigarette and gave it to her.

"Who are you?" she demanded.

"Gordy was blackmailing me."

She closed her eyes, nursing her glass.

"Oh no . . . not again," she muttered. "So what are you going to do? Burn me?" She let the glass slip out of her hand. It bounced on the tatty wool rug and the gin and water made a little puddle. She cradled her head in her hands and began to moan.

I moved away from her and sat in a chair. I waited, silent.

"Hell! I'm starting to live like a hog," she said as if speaking to herself. She got up, picked up the glass and went into the kitchen. She came back with a drink that would have felled an ox.

"You still here? I told you to take the breeze."

"I need your help."

She peered at me. Then she took a gulp from the glass. "Help?"

"That's right. My wife stole a bottle of perfume from the Welcome store," I said, speaking slowly and distinctly. "She got caught on the scanners. Gordy wanted twenty thousand for the strip of film. He's dead now, but the film is somewhere. I was hoping you would tell me where to find it."

With an unsteady hand, she put the glass on the night table.

"Jesse was a sonofabitch, but he got to me." The gin was working on her now. "I don't know how many times I told him to cut out this blackmail caper, but he wouldn't listen. I kept telling him it would land him in trouble. He wouldn't listen." She peered at me. "Judas! Am I drunk! Get the hell away from me! Leave me alone." She reached for the glass, knocked it over and again there was a puddle on the rug.

I sat still, watching her.

She said the usual four letter words, then she held her head in her hands again.

I remained still.

After some minutes, she looked up and glared at me.

"Look at this!" She flicked her wrap aside and showed me the burn. "That bastard came here and he burned me. He too wanted the film. So go ahead and burn me and see where it gets you!"

"Who was it?" I spoke gently, as if I were talking to someone who had just had a major operation.

"How would I know? A cop. I can smell a cop a mile away. A big bastard: blue, staring eyes. If I had been his mother I would have drowned him as soon as he had popped out."

I looked at the dead cigar and it jelled. Herman Webber! No regular cop would have burnt her.

"You gave him the film?"

She suddenly dropped backwards across the bed, putting her arm across her eyes.

"I want a drink."

I picked up the glass and went into the kitchen. I made a drink and came back. Then putting the glass on the night table, I picked her up and laid her on the bed with her head on the pillow.

"Going to start burning me?" she asked, but she smiled for the first time.

"Won't you help me?" I said, looking down at her. "Did you give him the film?"

"I told him where he could find it." She gave a drunken giggle. "I said I had mailed it to my sister in New York."

"Did you?"

"No."

"He's a cop, baby. He'll call your sister and he'll know she hasn't got it and he'll be back."

"She'll tell him yes and when he gets there, she'll spit in his eye. My sister and I work together."

"But he'll be back."

"I'll be the hell away from here by the time he does."

"I want that film. Would fifteen hundred dollars buy it for me?"

She studied me. Maybe this was a mistake because there came into her eyes an expression only a greedy hooker has.

"Come again?" she lifted her head. "How much?"

"Fifteen hundred. It could get you away from here. Do you know where the film is?"

She caught hold of my wrist.

"You mean you'll give me fifteen hundred bucks for the film?"

"That's what I mean."

She blew out her cheeks. The gin was now hitting her

hard and I began to wonder uneasily if she was going to pass out.

"I know where it is. You give me the money and you get it."

She reached for the drink, but I took it out of her hand.

"Skip it baby! You're already floating."

She nodded.

"Yeah . . . gimme a cigarette."

I lit one for her and watched her try to get hold of herself.

"Where is it?" I said.

"Anxious?" she smiled. "I know. Let's have the money first, buster. That's what Jesse always said to me: money first."

"The money is in the bank. You won't get it until tomorrow. You won't get it until I get the film. I want it now!"

"Then tomorrow we go to the bank, get the money and I'll give you the film. How's that, buster?"

"If that's the way you want to play it. By tomorrow you could be dead. That ex-cop isn't the only one after the film. There's a killer after it. Okay, if you want a bullet as Gordy got a bullet. we'll wait until tomorrow." I got up. "Can I use your phone? I want to call a cab."

She was sitting up now, her eyes scared.

"Hey! Wait a minute! What's this about a killer?"

"Your pal Gordy had a film that could put a lot of rich women in jail," I said. "Someone—probably a husband—tried to get the film and he shot Gordy. It could be your turn next. Consider yourself lucky that an ex-cop burnt you. Your next visitor could kill you."

I went over to the telephone and called a cab service. They said a cab would arrive in ten minutes.

I heard scuffling and looked over my shoulder to see Freda climbing into a dress. She was acting like she was about to miss a train.

"No need to panic, baby. You've forgotten your pants."

"I'm coming with you! I'm not staying here alone!"

"You don't come with me. You lock the door when I've

gone. Maybe this killer won't kick it down. See you . . ." and I went into the living-room.

She rushed after me.

"I'll give it to you. Honest! Can I come with you?"

She was now a frightened child who had got at the gin bottle.

"Okay . . . come on then. You've forgotten your shoes."

"You won't run out on me?"

"Get your shoes and your pants on. I'll wait."

She peered blearily at me.

"What do I want pants for?"

* * *

The cab dropped us outside the Imperial hotel. We transferred to my car.

She leaned against me as I started the motor.

"I'm trusting you," she said. "I'll give you the film, but you will give me the money, won't you?"

"Boy scout's honour."

She giggled. She was still very drunk.

"This is the first time I've ever trusted any man in my whole life."

"You have to begin sometime, baby."

I looked at the dashboard clock. The time was 23.15. Even though it was late, I wasn't risking driving up to Gordy's house. Goldstein could have a cop staked out there.

My garage doors were open. I drove the Merc straight in, got out, shut the doors turned on the light as Freda came weaving out.

"Where's this?" she asked, clutching hold of my arm.

"My home. Come on in. I'll get you a drink."

"That's talking."

I unlocked the door into the house and together we moved into the living-room.

"Hey!" She weaved and peered. "This is nice."

"Sit down."

I led her to a chair and parked her. She lay back, staring around.

I pulled the curtains, then fixed her a mild gin and tonic.

"Let's talk, baby," I said, sitting close to her. "Just relax and tell me about Gordy."

"What about him? He's dead."

"That's right. How did you meet him?"

"Last summer. Why should you care?" She sipped her drink, then put the glass on the occasional table by her. "He had got this job at the stores. His wife had left him. He had a little money. A guy needs a woman from time to time. We clicked. There was something about him that got to me. He was always talking about what he would do if he could get hold of big money." She grimaced. "Most men talk that way. Then one night while we were in bed, he told me about this scanner thing. He said he could raise a million dollars. We were both pretty drunk, but he seemed so sure."

"A million dollars?"

"That's what he said. I told him he was crazy, but he kept on and on. Then I got scared. I told him he could run into trouble. He knew that. He said he had a lot of little suckers on the film, but the scanner had caught a big one as well. He said the pay off would be a million. He said if I would help him, as soon as he got the money, we would take off and we'd settle together." She peered at me. "I'm shooting off, aren't I?"

"You're doing all right," I said. I was thinking fast. The only man living on Eastlake who could pay out a million was Creeden. A million. *A lot of little suckers and a big one!* So, suppose Gordy had caught ten little suckers, including me and Brenner. That could give him two hundred thousand. Creeden could be good for eight. If that wasn't a motive to kill Gordy what was? "How did you help him?"

"He wanted to spread the risk. He kept the film and he gave me the blow-ups."

"You have them?"

"Have I hell! How was I to know anyone would bust into my place? Okay, I drink. I'm a careless bitch. I didn't take all this talk about a million seriously. Jesse gave me a parcel and told me to hide it. I shoved it in a drawer and forgot about it. Then the night he died, I remembered

113

it and looked for it and it was gone. I blew my stupid
mind and I telephoned him, but there was no answer. I
drove over to his house and found him dead." She grimaced and reached for the glass.

That jelled. I remembered when I was standing over
Gordy's body, the telephone had rung.

"Did he tell you who the big sucker was?"

She sipped, put down the glass, then shook her head.

"No."

I got to my feet.

"I'm going to change. You sit still. Later, I'll go to
Gordy's house." I paused, then asked as casually as I could,
"Where do I find the film?"

She studied me, her eyes trying to focus.

"You're going to give me the money?"

"Boy scout's honour."

"Fifteen hundred bucks?"

"Boy scout's honour."

"Will you swear by your mother's grave you will give
me the money?"

"Boy scout's honour is better."

She thought about this, then nodded.

"Okay . . . always the sucker. It's in the bottom drawer
of his desk."

I stared at her.

"Don't give me that crap! The police would have
looked there!"

She shook her head.

"Jesse was smart. There's a false bottom. He had a
cabinet maker fix it. There's a hidden catch under the
desk. That's where it is."

I left her, took a shower and changed into dark casuals.
It was worth a try.

The time was just after midnight.

I armed myself with a small powerful flashlight and a
heavy screwdriver. I returned to the living-room. She was
sleeping. She had dropped her glass and there was a small
puddle of gin and water by her.

I left her, and headed for Gordy's house.

seven

I APPROACHED Gordy's house with stealth pausing every twenty yards to listen and peer into the gloom. No one was walking his dog. I passed two houses still emitting the sound of television. I was tense, wondering if I was going to walk into a cop. When I was in sight of the house, I stepped off the road and got behind a tree. I watched and waited.

There were no signs of life. I didn't hurry. I had plenty of time. After some fifteen minutes, I began to assure myself that there was no cop around so I moved out of my cover and cautiously reached the house. There was no light showing. Was there a cop sitting in the living-room in the dark? Moving silently, I stepped onto the small grass lawn and made my way around to the back of the house. Here, I paused and surveyed the scene: there was nothing to survey, so nerving myself, I moved up to the back door. It was locked of course. The police wouldn't have left it unlocked that was why I had brought the screwdriver.

A quick look at the lock in the light of my flash showed me it was flimsy. I inserted the screwdriver and levered gently. After a little more pressure the lock sprang and the door opened. There had been a minimum of noise. I didn't move into the darkness, but stood, listening. I only heard the thump of my heartbeats. I turned on my flash, found I was in a small kitchen, entered and closed the door. I eased open the kitchen door, paused to listen again, then sent the beam of my flash down the short corridor which

115

ended at the front door. I remembered the living-room lay to my left.

I moved silently down the corridor until I reached the living-room door which was closed. I hesitated. If a cop was sitting in there, waiting, I would be in real trouble. As I stood, sweating, I told myself I would be in more trouble if I didn't get the film.

I turned the handle and opened the door. Faint moonlight came through the big window. I looked around. No one sprang at me. No bawling cop voice challenged me. I moved into the room, closing the door and fumbled my way to the window. I pulled the flimsy curtains. I couldn't risk turning on the electric light.

I located the desk. It stood in a corner. I crossed to it, knelt and examined the underneath in the light of my flash. It took me several seconds to find a tiny wooden knob. If Freda hadn't told me, I would have missed it.

I pulled open the bottom drawer which was full of account books and old check stubs. I scooped these onto the floor, then reaching under the desk, I pressed the knob. The bottom of the drawer moved back four inches and there lying in the hollow was a carton of 16 mm. film.

I knelt there, staring at it, scarcely believing my eyes, then I snatched it up and put it on the desk. I pressed the knob again, closing the partition, then carefully returned the junk I had spilled on the floor.

Picking up the carton, I moved fast to the door and into the corridor.

Maybe he had been in the house all the time or maybe he had been hiding in the garden and had followed me in. That's something I didn't discover.

As I reached the back door, clutching the carton, I heard a tiny rustle behind me. As I was turning, much too late, a light seemed to explode inside my head and I was down on hands and knees. There was a vague flicker of light, then the sounds of running feet.

I remained still, my head trying to burst, then with an effort I supported myself against the wall, my eyes closed, while my head screamed at me. After some moments the screaming died down and I felt the back of my head. There was a small bump. The blow hadn't been vicious, but bad enough.

I groped around on the floor, found my flashlight and turned it on. I made sure the carton of film had gone. Then with a feeling of sick despair, I tottered out into the warm night air.

It took me nearly twenty minutes to get to the end of East Avenue. I kept losing my balance like a drunk and twice I had to sit on the grass verge, then the night air or something cleared my throbbing head and I was able to walk straight and I walked straight into Mark Creeden and his dog.

"Well, for God's sake!" he exploded. "Are you working out another problem?"

"That's it." My voice was husky. "Always problems."

He laughed.

"You're right. I have a problem with this pooch. Look at the time! At my age . . . dog walking after midnight."

I tried to see his face but, it was too dark. Was this the man who had killed Gordy? Was this the man who had just hit me over the head and had taken the film?

"I hear you're leaving Eastlake, Manson. I'm sorry. I'm sorry too about the break-up."

"Thank you." My head was throbbing badly now. I was in no mood for chit-chat. "Well, I'll go along."

I started off again and he fell into step.

"May as well go back myself."

We walked in silence for some yards, then he said, "Do you think we're going to be blackmailed again, Manson?"

"I don't know."

"Someone must have this goddamn film."

If you haven't, I thought.

"Yes."

A long pause as we walked side by side.

"Haven't you, with your connections, some way of finding it?"

"Haven't you?"

"I'm trying."

"It affects both you and me, Manson. Do more than try. If Goldstein finds the film, we're both in serious trouble.

I've already lied to him. Tomorrow, it'll be your turn."

We had now reached my house.

"I understand Mitchell's parents are taking over your house," Creeden said as I opened the gate.

"That's right."

"We should keep in touch. Where are you going to live?"

"I'm looking around. When I find some place, I'll telephone you." My head was giving me hell. All I wanted now was to get away from him.

"Do that. Try for the film and watch Goldstein."

"Sure."

I walked up the drive, leaving him standing by the gate, his spaniel by him.

As I unlocked the front door, I remembered I had Freda Hawes in my living-room. I entered silently, shut and locked the door, then looked into the living-room. She was still there, still asleep.

I went into the kitchen, broke open a tray of ice cubes, collected a number in a towel and applied them to the bump on my head. After a while, the raging headache diminished. I looked at my watch. The time was 01.10. I was now able to think. An odd time for a man as rich as Creeden to walk his dog. Had it been Creeden? I hoped it was for I was sure Creeden would destroy the film. But was it Creeden?

I heard sounds from the living-room.

"Who's there?" Freda's voice was shrill.

"It's me."

I braced myself, then dropping the ice cubes in the sink, I walked into the living-room.

She was sitting straight up in the chair, her eyes pools of terror, but when she saw me, she relaxed.

"Hell! You scared the pants right off me!" she said.

"Remember? You're not wearing pants." I went to the liquor cabinet and poured myself a shot of scotch. "You want a drink?"

"No."

This startled me. I looked at her. She had become sober and there was a hard expression on her face that should have warned me.

"You got it, huh? Just like I said?" She leaned forward, staring at me. "So now you give me the money, huh?"

I drank half the whisky and then put down the glass. I was still feeling pretty shaky, but I was alert enough to know I had yet another problem on my hands.

I came over and sat close to her.

"I went over there and got the film," I said.

"So I get the money, huh?"

She nodded.

"Are you sober enough to get to your feet?"

She stared at me. The drunken peer had gone.

"What the hell are you saying?"

She stood up and moved to me.

"Give me your hand."

"What's this, buster?"

"Give me your hand."

She held out her hand and I took it, then guided it to the back of my head.

"Feel, but carefully."

Her fingers crossed over the growing egg on the back of my head, then she shoved my head forward and peered. She hurt, but I let her look. She drew in a hissing breath and moved away from me.

"What's that?"

"I got the film, but someone was there and he hit me solid. He now has the film."

She flew into a rage that shocked me. Standing over me she screamed filth.

"Boy scout's honour!" she finally yelled. "I knew it! You're lying! You give me the money! Hear me? Fifteen hundred! I'm going to have it!"

Her screaming voice could have been heard half way down the avenue. I couldn't believe any women could make such an uproar. I suddenly realised that someone in this quiet avenue might be calling the police.

Reaching forward, I jabbed my thumb into her tummy, hard. Her screaming voice cut as if I had snapped off a radio programme. She staggered back, her mouth as big as a fire bucket, over-balanced and sat down on the floor with a spine-jarring thud.

"Do you want the cops here, you stupid bitch?" I said.

She held her tummy and stared up at me.

"If they come here, you're in trouble. Get up, sit down and shut up!"

She sat there, trying to get her breath. Finally, as I made no move to help her, she crawled to her feet, her hands cupping her buttocks.

"You bastard! You've broken my spine!" But her voice was low. She staggered to a chair and sank into it, moaning.

I lit a cigarette and waited. She took some minutes to start thinking again.

"You wouldn't kid me?" she asked finally. "Someone took the film?"

"Do you imagine I would knock myself on the head?"

She brooded about this, then nodded.

"Well, the creep has the little suckers, but he hasn't got the big one."

"What do you mean?"

"There are two films. The one you lost isn't worth much. The other one could be worth a million bucks." She stared thoughtfully at me. "Suppose you and me work together, buster? You take a quarter. I take the rest. How's about it?"

At that moment the front door bell rang.

* * *

I grabbed hold of Freda's arm, jerked her to her feet and rushed her into my bedroom.

"Stay still and quiet!" I said, then shutting the door I went to the front door and opened it as the bell rang again.

In Eastlake you get cop service. Someone had telephoned and within minutes the cops had arrived.

Standing on my doorstep was a big, bulky cop and by the gate was a younger, less bulky cop.

"What's going on?" The big cop regarded me, his hand fingering his pistol holster. I recognised him.

"Hello there, Flynn. What do you mean?"

He stared stonily at me.

"We had a call, Mr. Manson. A woman screaming."

"Come in," I said. "I'm sorry. My goddamn radio is on the blink. I was listening to the late night horror."

He moved and entered the living-room.

"I was in my bedroom with the volume turned up and the radio went haywire. The sound nearly knocked my ears off." I forced a grin. "Sorry if I've caused a disturbance."

He regarded me, his little eyes suspicious.

"I was told a woman was in trouble."

"There's no woman here."

"Your radio, huh?"

"That's right. I'll get it fixed tomorrow."

He looked at the set and I knew he was itching to turn it on, but he also knew I was the editor of *The Voice of the People*.

"Okay," he said. "You caused an alarm, Mr. Manson."

"It alarmed me, too."

"A horror programme, huh?"

He could check this, but there was no other way out.

"That's it."

He nodded.

"Pretty late to listen to the radio, Mr. Manson."

"Is there a law against it?" I stared him eyeball to eyeball and he decided I was a heavyweight against his lightweight.

"Well, it's plenty late."

He looked around the lounge, saw the puddle of gin and water, saw my half-finished drink, saw Freda's empty glass. This cop was nobody's fool.

"I'm sleeping badly," I said.

He nodded, then made for the front door.

"And thanks, sergeant, for coming so quickly," I said.

He gave me a cold, cop stare as he said, "That's my job."

I watched him walk down the drive, join the other cop, watched him pause and talk. They got in their car.

Freda came out of my bedroom.

"You played that smooth, buster," she said. "I'm beginning to respect you."

"As if you could respect anyone. You wouldn't know the meaning of the word. Go back in there."

She lifted her eyebrows.

"Getting that feeling, buster? Sure, the bedroom is my territory."

She went into the bedroom. I turned off the lights in the sitting-room, then lifted the heavy curtains aside and saw the police car was still there. After some minutes it drove away.

My head still throbbed, but not badly enough to prevent me from thinking. Two films! The film that had been stolen would reveal those stupid women—like Linda—stealing, but the second film could and probably did show someone like Mabel Creeden stealing and there was the big money. There too was the reason for murder: why Gordy had been shot. Thinking about it, as I stood in the darkness, by the window, I realised the second film—worth a million dollars in blackmail money—could be more important now to me than the film I had lost. It would nail the killer.

I went into the bedroom.

It was strange to see this woman lying in the bed I had shared for some time with Linda. She had the sheet over her. The bedside lamp made shadows in the room.

"Let's forget today, buster," she said. "Come on. Let's have some action."

The bedside clock showed 01.35. My head still ached. I was tired, but not that tired.

I sat on the bed and looked at her.

"What's this about a second film?"

"Man! Are you a sucker for punishment!" She threw aside the sheet so I could see her naked body. "Strip off and relax."

I pulled the sheet over her.

"What's this about a second film?"

"Oh, go to hell! I want to sleep. Go away if you don't want to keep me company!"

"What's this about a million dollars?"

Her eyes lit up.

"Are you interested? A quarter for you, the rest for me?"

"Why not?"

"No. You're not the type. You wouldn't blackmail, would you?"

"Would you?"

"For that kind of bread." She stared up at the ceiling. "A million bucks! Think what you could do with it!"

If I could only con her to tell me where the film was!

"Yes . . . that's real money. What do we do?"

"I've got the film. Jesse was scared of it. He gave it to me to keep. He said he could handle the little suckers on the other film, but it would need the two of us to swing the big one."

"So you have it? Where is it?"

"I have it so that makes me worth a million bucks."

She lifted her arms above her head and smiled at me.

"That's the sixty-four thousand dollar question, buster."

"Unless you get shot like Gordy did, then you're worth nothing."

"Whoever shot Jesse didn't get the film. Whoever shoots me won't get it either. It's stashed away and safe."

"Who's the big sucker on the film?"

"He didn't tell me, but she's on the film. Jesse told me that. I have only to run off the film to know her."

She thought about this, then nodded.

"There's that. Yeah . . . there are so many rich bitches around."

"But I would know her. It's part of my job to know everyone with money in this city. Suppose you and I work together? Where's the film?"

"I'll think about it. You could have a point, buster. Do you want to join me in bed?"

. I stood up. The time was 01.40. My head still ached.

"Not tonight."

She looked relieved.

"Then fade away. I want to sleep."

I left her and bedded down in the spare bedroom. I tried to sleep, but thoughts kept churning through my mind. Finally, I got up, went into the bathroom and took a pill . . . a mistake.

The sound of the telephone bell brought me awake. I looked at the bedside clock. The time, to my consternation, was 09.35. My head still felt sore, but it no longer ached. I grabbed up the reciever.

"Steve?" It was Jean. "Are you all right?"

I tried to gather what wits I had left.

"I'm okay ... I've overslept."

"Mr. Chandler is asking for you."

"Tell him I'll be right over."

"You have an appointment with Larry Hersche at ten."

Hersche was our artist and not important.

"Put him off." I got out of bed. "What's the mail like?"

"It's heavy."

"Okay, Jean, I'll be with you," and I hung up.

Then I remembered I had Freda still in my hair. She couldn't stay here. It was Cissy's afternoon to clean. I went into the main bedroom expecting to find Freda still asleep, but the bed was empty. I looked around, then went into the kitchen. A used coffee cup stood on the sink.

"Freda?"

No answer. I went through the house, but she had gone. I dunked my face in cold water, shaved, then hurried back to the spare bedroom. I made the bed. I could leave the main bedroom for Cissy to fix. It wouldn't do for her to find both bedrooms had been used. As I threw on my clothes, I wondered where Freda had got to. Surely, she hadn't walked down to the taxi rank which was a good half-mile from my house.

The solution came when I went into the garage. She had taken Linda's Mini. I returned to the house, looked up her number and called her. There was a delay, then she answered.

"This is me," I said. "No names. What's going on?"

"I'm packing and getting out." She sounded breathless.

"You have my car."

"Oh, sure. It's parked on 22nd Street. The key's under the mat. Listen, buster, I need a getaway stake. Meet me at The Annex on 12th Street at nine tonight and bring me fifteen hundred bucks. We'll talk business," and she hung up.

I put down the reciever, went to the front door as a police car pulled up. I paused, seeing Lieutenant Goldstein get out. I shut the door, locked it as he came up the drive.

"Can you spare a minute, Mr. Manson?"

"Not right now, Leiutenant. I've overslept and in a hurry to get to Mr. Chandler who is calling for me."

He eyed me, his expression wooden.

"We could talk as you drove."

"Okay."

I opened the garage doors, backed the Merc out and he got in. As I drove down the avenue, I saw in my driving mirror the police car was following.

"What's on your mind, Lieutenant?" I asked as I moved into the flow of traffic.

"The Gordy killing. I have reason to believe that a number of people living on the Eastlake estate have been shoplifting. The store has installed scanners. The master scanner ran a 16 mm. film. Gordy's hobby appears to have been photography. There's no film in the store: no film in his house. It points to blackmail."

"I can see that." I made my voice disinterested.

"Yes. I'm talking to everyone who used the store. Did you?"

"No."

"Your wife?"

"Yes."

A pause, then he asked, "Regularly?"

"I think so."

I had my eyes on the road. The traffic was heavy. I didn't have to look at him.

"I would like to talk to her. She might give me ideas."

"I doubt that."

"When can I see her?"

"She's in Dallas right now."

"Well, that's not on the moon. I'd be glad if you will give me her address in Dallas."

"I see no point in bothering her. I'm sure she won't be able to help you."

"This is a murder inquiry, Mr. Manson."

I knew I was licked.

"I'm terrible about addresses. I have it written down. I'll call you."

"If you will do that, Mr. Manson."

We were now driving along the highway, heading for the city.

"Mr. Manson, I like to be fed ideas," Goldstein said. "You are a trained journalist. What do you think? I can't see a woman walking into Gordy's house and shooting him, but I can see a husband of a woman who has been stealing and is being blackmailed doing just that. What do you think?"

"Sounds reasonable."

A long silence as we entered the city, then he said, "There was a complaint last night about a woman screaming in your house."

"I sorted that out with Patrolman officer Flynn," I said. "My radio is on the blink."

Another long silence, then as I pulled into a parking bay outside Chandler's block, Goldstein said, "I have to listen to gossip, Mr. Manson. Is it correct that you and your wife are parting?"

I faced him.

"It is correct but I don't see it is any business of yours."

"Sure." He nodded. "You will let me have her address?"

"Yes."

He studied me, his grey eyes like gimlets.

"Perhaps the screaming woman last night wasn't the radio, Mr. Manson?"

I had had enough of him.

"Don't bet on it, Lieutenant. As long as Mr. Chandler is my boss, don't bet on anything regarding me."

It was the best I could do, but it held him. I left him, rubbing his hooked nose and staring into space.

*　　　*　　　*

As I walked into Chandler's office, I could see he was in a bad mood. There was that deep wrinkle between his heavy eyebrows that was the danger signal.

"Sit down. What's this I hear about you and Linda?"

I was in no mood to be browbeaten.

"Linda and I have decided to divorce," I said, sitting down. "It happens every hour of every day."

He glowered at me.

"I warned you. In your position, you can't afford to run this magazine and have a scandal."

My head began to ache again and I suddenly didn't give a damn. I had a hundred and thirty thousand dollars in the bank. I could go back to Los Angeles and start again as a columnist.

"You warned me, Mr. Chandler," I said. "So I'll resign. How's that?"

He leaned forward.

"You serious, Steve?"

"I'm serious," I said. "If I can't get a divorce without you getting on a high horse, then I'll quit."

His glower went away.

"That's the last thing you're going to do." He took a cigar from the box on his desk, cut and lit it, then he went on, "If you quit, Steve, the magazine would fold. You're doing a fine job. Is there another woman?"

It was time to give it to him straight.

"Yes. There's another woman. Linda has got hooked with a middle-aged, ugly dyke. I haven't any woman."

He blew out his cheeks, studied his cigar, then grimaced.

"You shock me, Steve."

"Can you imagine what it has done to me?"

"Turn a stone and find a worm, huh?"

"It is easy to criticise."

He drew more smoke from the cigar, then shrugged.

"Hammond says he is going to sue."

"That's what we want, isn't it?"

Chandler nodded.

"But he won't. The cards are stacked."

"Is that all, Mr. Chandler? I have work to do."

He regarded me, then nodded.

"You're doing a fine job, Steve. I'm sorry about this thing. I want you to know I'm behind you."

"Thanks." I got to my feet. "Well . . ."

"We must do something about Wally Mitford. When he's fit, I want him in the sun."

I was already halfway across his office. I stopped short.

"Wally is already in Miami."

He looked surprised.

"Is that right?" He shook his head. "That Borg! He's always three jumps ahead of the gun. Good." He waved his cigar at me. "Keep going, Steve. Try to forget your troubles. I've already forgotten them."

I left him on that note.

Back in my office, I coped with the mail, discussed with Jean the layout for Rafferty's article, then settled down to the routine grind. I told Jean I would have a desk lunch and she got Judy to organise sandwiches for me. She said she had a lunch date, but would be back at 14.00. I wondered if she was lunching with her boy-friend. Again, as she left my office, I felt a little pang.

I had the office to myself so I put a call through to Dallas.

Mrs. Lucas—Linda's mother—answered. As soon as I made myself known, she said, as Linda and I were going to get a divorce, was it wise for me to talk to her?

I said it was and after a delay, Linda came on the line.

"Lieutenant Goldstein wants to question you," I said. "He's a toughie. I suggest you and Lucilla take off for a trip around Mexico. Stay away and out of his reach for at least two months." Before she could start bleating, I hung up.

I was sure Lucilla, who was no one's fool, would see the red light, and by the evening, they would be on their way. Linda's mother was rich enough to finance the trip.

I was eating my second sandwich when Max Berry breezed in.

"Look, Steve, I have an idea," he said, dropping into the chair by my desk. "How's about me going after Senator

Linsky? That old crook has been feathering his nest for years. I've got a lead on him that could shoot him up to the moon."

"Okay, Max. See what you can dig up."

He rubbed his hand around his face, hesitated, then said, "You know how it is, Steve . . . talk. About Linda . . .?"

I froze, thinking: is it geting around she is a thief?

"What about her?"

"Well, you and she . . ." He shifted uneasily. "Not my business, of course."

"That's okay." I relaxed. "Yes, we're parting. That reminds me. You had better have my new address." I scribbled the address and the telephone number on a scratch pad and handed it to him. "I'll be moving in tomorrow."

"Fine." He looked at the address, then at me. "Did Borg fix this for you?"

"Borg! No, Jean did."

"This is one of Borg's apartments."

I stared at him.

"Does Borg own apartments?"

"Sure. He's smart. He's put most of his money in bricks and cement."

"I didn't know. Well, okay, Max, see what you can dig up about Linsky."

He said he would and left me.

I sat for some moments staring down at my cluttered desk. Borg again? Once more I felt as if someone was breathing down the back of my neck.

The telephone bell snapped me out of my thinking and for the next hour I was kept busy.

Jean returned. I asked her if she had had a good lunch and she nodded: no information forthcoming. When she began typing, I remembered Freda Hawes. She had asked for fifteen hundred dollars. Maybe she would give me the film. I wrote a cheque, looked in on Jean, telling her I was going across to the bank. I collected fifteen one-hundred dollar bills. Ernie came out of his office and beamed at me.

"What are you going to do with all that money, Steve?"

he asked as he shook hands. "How about investing it? Dow Jones is flat on its back right now. It's a good time."

"Yeah. I'll come and see you. You might get some ideas down on paper, Ernie."

"Sorry about Linda."

"Yes. Well, see you," and I returned to the office.

I was kept busy until 18.00, then things quieted down. I remembered to call police headquarters. I asked to speak to Lieutenant Goldstein. Whoever took the call said he was out. I told him who I was and that my wife could be reached at 1113, Westside, Dallas. I was told the lieutenant would be informed. By the time Goldstein got busy, Linda and Lucilla would be lost in Mexico. At least that was one problem solved.

I decided I had had enough for the day. I could hear Jean's typewriter clacking. I cleared my desk and went into her office. She paused, looking at me.

"When are you moving in, Steve?"

"Maybe tonight. I didn't see the lease. Who owns the apartment?"

"Western Properties."

"Who are they?"

"Real estate people."

"Max tells me the apartment is owned by Joe Borg."

"That's right. He is in real estate as a sideline." She sat back. "Mr. Chandler wouldn't approve so it is confidential. I help Mr. Borg let some of his apartments. I knew this one was vacant. That was how I could fix you up so quickly."

We looked at each other. Her calm eyes told me nothing.

"Are you working late?" I asked.

"Another half an hour."

"Well, I'll get off home. There are still things I have to clear up."

"Goodnight, Steve."

"Goodnight."

I drove home, took a shower and changed into casuals. I walked around the house. I had no feeling for it now. It was no longer mine. In two days, Harry Mitchell's parents would be installed.

I spent the next hour cleaning up. Cissy had made a reasonable job of cleaning and she had cleared the refrigerator. I put my remaining clothes in a suitcase and dumped it into the back of the Merc.

I remembered that Freda had said she had parked the Mini on 22nd Street. I called a cab service. The cab took me to 22nd Street where I found the Mini. I drove it to an all-night car dealer and after haggling, he gave me less than a quarter of what it was worth.

The time now was 20.10. I spent half an hour in an Eat's bar, chewing on a hamburger and sipping a double scotch on the rocks. Then I remembered—it seemed I was always remembering—I had a date with Sergeant Brenner at the Half Moon bar at 21.00. I looked up the number of the bar and called.

When a voice answered I said, "Jake?"

"Yeah."

"Tell Brenner not until ten o'clock."

"Okay," and the line went dead.

I finished my drink, then as I still had time to kill, I decided I would walk to 12th Street. I arrived at The Annex ten minutes before 21.00.

The Annex was one of those glossy bars with lots of mirrors, high stools, banquettes in semi-darkness, soft music and a barman with choppers a horse would envy.

The place was nearly empty. There were four couples supporting the bar: Young, well-dressed, bored looking. I glanced around. Freda hadn't arrived.

The barman showed me his teeth. I said a scotch on the rocks. When I got it, I carried it to one of the banquettes and sat down. I had a view of the entrance.

At 21.15, just as I was getting worried, Freda came in. She was wearing a light dust coat over an orange and red cotton dress. She carried an air travel bag, slung over her shoulder. She saw me and moved a little unsteadily to the banquette and sat down, facing me. She looked a little drunk.

"Mine's a double gin, straight." she said.

The barman came over, took the order, came back with the drink and placed it before her.

131

We waited until he had gone away, then Freda said, "I'm on my way, buster." She blew out her cheeks and fanned my face with gin fumes. "What a day! I've been chasing my goddamn tail until now. When a girl with my connections pulls out, she has one hell of a pull out, but never mind that." She leaned forward, staring at me. "But in spite of the rush, I've had time to think. Blackmail is not for me. It didn't do Jesse any good. Who wants a million if you land up in jail or you get a bullet the way he did? Give me the money and the film is yours. I've got it right here."

"You could be selling me any film, couldn't you?"

She drank half the gin, nodded, then poked an unsteady finger in my direction.

"Boy scout's honour."

"Okay. It's a deal."

"Let's have the bread, buster."

I looked around. No one was paying us any attention. I took the fifteen one-hundred dollar bills from my hip pocket and shoved the roll across the table. She snatched it up and stuffed it into her handbag. Then she zipped open her air travel bag and gave me a carton of 16 mm. film.

"That's it," she said. "I'm on my way to get lost. Watch it, buster. That film is loaded with trouble and I'm damn glad to be shot of it."

"Where are you going?"

"The moon won't be far enough." She swallowed her drink, shuddered, then slid out of the banquette. "If that film can fix the sonofabitch who killed Jesse, it'll make my day." With a brief nod, she was gone.

That was the last time I saw her.

eight

I⃟T⃟ ⃟W⃟A⃟S⃟ a little after 22.00 when I arrived at the Half Moon bar. When Freda had left me, I took a taxi to my bank where they had an all-night safe deposit service. The film she had given me had already caused Gordy's death. I wasn't taking any chances with it. It wasn't until I had locked it safely that I was able to relax. Sometime tomorrow I would hire a 16 mm. projector and take a look at the film.

I found Brenner nursing a beer in the upstairs room. He looked sourly at me as I shut the door.

"I'm on early duty," he said. "I've got to get some sleep. What's cooking?"

I sat at the table, facing him. I had to confide in someone and who better than a disinterested cop?

So I told him about Freda, about finding the film in Gordy's desk drawer, how I was slugged, how the film had gone missing, how she had told me there was a second film and it was now in my bank.

He sipped his beer, smoked, stared down at the table and listened. By the time I had finished, tiny sweat beads made his face glisten.

"Do you think Creeden's got it?"

"I hope so. If he has it, he'll destroy it."

He thought about this, then wiped his hand over his face. "As long as that film exists, we both are in trouble."

"I know that."

We stared at each other.

133

"What about this second film? When are you looking at it?"

"I'll hire a projector tomorrow."

"I want to see it."

"Who wouldn't?" I looked at the dirty white wall facing me. "I could bring the film and the projector here in my lunch hour."

He shook his head.

"I'm not off duty until four."

"Come to my new apartment?"

Again he shook his head.

"I'll tell you something, Manson. Goldstein has his eye on you. Watch it. You could be tailed. If he saw you and me together, it would sink me."

"So what do we do?"

He thought about this, then said, "I'll check if you're being tailed. Give me your telephone number. If you're in the clear, I'll call you around midnight. I'll say 'Roger' and hang up. If you're being tailed, I won't call. If you aren't, we meet here tomorrow night. Bring the film and projector . . . right?"

"Okay."

He lit another cigarette and brooded for a moment, then he said, "Let's look at this set-up. Let's run through the suspects. There's you, me, Creeden and Latimer. Your gun killed the creep so that puts you way ahead of the rest. I'm thinking as Goldstein would think. But if this hustler is giving it to you straight, the second film is the money-maker so that puts Creeden who has that kind of money in the photo . . . right?"

I thought about Creeden. He was rich, tough and ruth-less: not a man who would stand for blackmail. If his wife had been stealing and if Gordy tried to squeeze him for something like a million dollars, Creeden could turn killer. He had had the opportunity of stealing my gun, shooting Gordy and returning it.

But how did he know I had the gun?

I asked Brenner.

"Pistol permits have to be cleared in this city by an

acting magistrate," Brenner told me. "That's what Creeden is."

"His signature wasn't on the permit."

"He doesn't sign it. It's a matter of form. He okays it and the Chief of Police signs it."

"So he would have known I had the gun."

"Yeah."

"I ran into him coming away from Gordy's house on the night of the murder. I ran into him when I got knocked on the head and lost the film. Damn it! It points to Creeden."

Brenner showed his teeth in a cynical smile.

"Try to prove it."

I scribbled down my new telephone number and gave it to him.

"I'm going back to my apartment now. Call me."

"If you don't hear from me by midnight, you're being tailed."

Leaving the Half Moon bar, I walked to the end of the street before I found a taxi. I gave the driver my new address and looked through the rear window to see if I could spot anyone following me. At this hour traffic was heavy. All I saw was a mass of cars behind the cab. Again I had a feeling of someone breathing down the back of my neck and I felt very alone.

When the cab stopped outside my apartment block, I paid the cabby, then took the elevator up to my new home. I turned on the light and looked around. Strange surroundings and again I felt lonely.

Whoever Jean had found to arrange things in the apartment had done a good job. There was even a vase of roses on an occasional table, but they didn't help me.

I went into the bedroom, stripped off my jacket, dropped it on the bed, then went into the bathroom and washed my hands. Was this going to be my future life? I wondered, drying my hands on a towel. Alone? I thought of Jean. If she had been here, how the scene would have changed! How wonderful it would be!

I wandered back into the living-room and sat down. I

now thought of the film I had locked away in the safe deposit box. If, when I ran it off, it showed Mabel Creeden stealing, what was I going to do? Hand it over to Goldstein? Thinking about this, I decided no. Creeden, fighting back, could involve me too and Linda's stealing would be exposed. At the moment, Chandler was leaning over backwards for me, but I was sure he would give me the gate if Linda's stealing became news.

I would keep the film as an insurance. Someone had the reel of tape with Gordy's voice threatening me with blackmail. This someone probably had the film showing Linda stealing. If this someone was Creeden, then he would hold onto this evidence in case Goldstein caught up with him. A clever defence attorney could shift the killing on to me.

I looked at my watch. The time was now 23.20. I would sit up until midnight, hoping Brenner would call. I lit a cigarette and tried to relax, but thoughts kept moving through my mind.

Then the front door bell rang.

I stiffened, hesitated, and after a long moment, I got to my feet, went into the lobby and opened the door.

Lieutenant Goldstein stood in the corridor. Behind him was a bulky man with cop written all over him.

"I saw your light, Mr. Manson," Goldstein said smoothly. "May we come in? This is Sergeant Hammer."

I stood aside.

"I was just going to bed, Lieutenant, but come in. Can I offer you a drink?"

"No, thank you." He entered the living-room, glanced around, nodded as if with approval. "Nice place you have here."

"Just moved in. How did you know where to find me?"

He moved to a chair and sat down. Hammer went to the table and sat by it.

"We have ways and means," Goldstein said and smiled his thin smile. "I tried to contact your wife, Mr. Manson. Apparently she is touring Mexico."

"Is she? I'm arranging a divorce, Lieutenant. Frankly, I couldn't care less where my wife is right at this moment."

I sat on the arm of a lounging chair.

136

"Is that what you wanted to see me about?" I asked, after a long pause.

"No . . . no . . ." He regarded me, his little eyes probing. "That gun of yours still worries me, Mr. Manson. When it was issued to Mr. Borg for you there was a box of slugs to go with it . . . fifty slugs. Right?"

I felt a slight tension.

"That is correct."

"You still have the box of slugs?"

"Yes."

"They should have been returned."

"In the confusion of the move here, I forgot them. If you will tell me to whom I should return them, I will do so."

"We won't bother you with that. Let me have them now."

"You don't mean you have come here at half past eleven to collect a box of cartridges, Lieutenant?"

"I would like the slugs!" There was a cop snap in his voice.

I shrugged and went to a closet. After a search, I found the box and handed it to him. He in turn handed it to Hammer who examined the cartridges.

"Six missing," he said in a hard, flat voice.

"I loaded the gun," I explained. "If you remember, the gun was stolen. The cartridges went with the gun."

"Yes." Goldstein stared down at his hands. "Mr. Manson, are you acquainted with Freda Hawes?" He looked up sharply and his eyes probed. It was a sucker punch and it had me floundering for a brief second as he meant it to do.

"Yes."

I was back on even keel now, but the damage was done. Creeden had warned me about Goldstein. He had slipped in a mean one and he had got his reaction.

"When did you last see her, Mr. Manson."

I felt it time to assert myself.

"Why should I answer that question, Lieutenant?"

He leaned forward, staring intently at me.

"She was shot dead this evening. A cartridge case, matching these issued to you, was found by her side. I have reason to believe the gun that killed her also killed Gordy: the gun you allege was stolen from your car. So I ask again, when did you last see her?"

* * *

A long silence built up in the room while I stared at Goldstein. I felt a chill crawl over me and I felt blood leaving my face.

He and Hammer watched me the way a cat watches a mouse.

"She's dead?" I finally managed to say.

"That's right. She's dead."

I hadn't lived in the tough newspaper world for nothing. Somehow I pulled myself together and got my mind working.

"Well, for God's sake!" I said. "I only saw her a couple of hours ago!"

"You saw her . . . two hours ago?"

"That's right." I was thinking fast now. "I'll explain. Ever since Gordy's killing, I have been wondering why someone should have killed him, as you have been. I edit a successful magazine. Gordy's killing is topical news so I decided I would investigate this blackmail angle you suggested to me. The only lead that looked promising was this woman: Freda Hawes. I wondered if she might tell me more than you, so I telephoned her. She was scared and planning to leave, but she wanted a get-away stake. She said she had information she would sell for fifteen hundred dollars. This sounded interesting. I got the money and met her at The Annex bar. We talked. She was half drunk and frightened. She said someone might kill her as Gordy was killed. She told me Gordy had a film showing a number of women, living at Eastlake, stealing and he had been black-mailing them. She wanted to know if she told me where the film was, would I give her money. I have had a lot of experience interviewing people and I was satisfied she meant business. I gave her the money and she told me the film was in a hidden compartment in Gordy's desk drawer. There is a little knob under the desk that releases the partition in the desk. We met at nine-fifteen and she left me twenty minutes later with the money. I was going to call you tomorrow to tell you to check the desk. I'm pretty sure when you do, you will find the film."

I saw Hammer was busy writing in his notebook. Goldstein, looking thoughtful, was stroking his hooked nose.

"What did you do, Mr. Manson, after she left you at nine-forty?"

Watch it, I told myself. I had to keep Brenner out of this.

"I went to the Half Moon bar," I said. "I arrived there just after ten."

"Why did you go there?"

"Looking for information. Freda Hawes mentioned that she used the bar. I was looking for background material. I talked to the barman, but she was either lying or he wasn't passing out information. I got nothing from him so I came back here."

He studied me, then nodded.

"You didn't think to tell me this when I arrived, Mr. Manson."

"You didn't give me much chance, did you?"

Again he studied me, then said. "You gave her fifteen hundred dollars for this information . . . in cash?"

"Yes. She put the money in her handbag. She was also carrying a Pan-Am over-night bag."

"When she was found, she had no handbag . . . no overnight bag."

"If you could find the film, Lieutenant, it could solve your problems."

"That's right." He rubbed his hooked nose and then got to his feet. He started to move to the door. Sergeant Hammer picked up the box of cartridges and started after him. Goldstein paused and stared at me. "Mr. Manson, it would help this investigation if you were frank with me. Was Gordy blackmailing you?"

"Suppose you wait until you get that film, Lieutenant?" I said. "If he was blackmailing me, I wasn't the only one."

"You will be seeing me again, Mr. Manson," he said and they went away.

I waited until I heard the elevator descend, then I sat in a chair, feeling shaky.

Goldstein hadn't been talking for the sake of hearing his own voice. He had said the gun that had killed Freda was the gun issued to me by Borg. He, like Brenner, had identified the cartridge case. Jean had told me she had dumped the gun in a sack of refuse. She and I had been satisfied the gun was lost, but it couldn't have been. For some time now I had the feeling that someone was breathing down my neck. Suppose that someone had followed me to Jean's place, then followed her, seen where she had dumped the gun and as soon as she had gone, had collected it? This could be the only explanation. Someone on the second film who was desperate to get that film. So desperate, he/she had been watching Freda. Seeing her with the Pan-Am bag he/she had decided she had the second film in the bag, shot her with the same ruthlessness as Gordy had been shot: using my gun.

I felt cold sweat on my face as I thought of this. It seemed more likely that the killer was the one who had broken in and taken the reel of tape that would hook me to Gordy's killing. It also pointed to him as the man who had hit me over the head and taken the first film.

My mind turned to Creeden. He fitted my picture of a ruthless killer. I looked at my watch. The time was five minutes to midnight. I knew the Creedens kept late hours. Crossing to the telephone, I called his number.

His wife, Mabel answered.

"Hello, Mabel, this is Steve Manson," I said. "Sorry to call so late. Is Mark there?"

"Mark is down town somewhere," she told me. "He should be back any moment now. He had a business dinner. I can't think what's keeping him."

"I just wanted a word, I'll call him tomorrow."

"Steve . . . I'm so sorry about Linda."

I had to listen to ten minutes of her yakking, but finally cut her short.

"Well, do come and see us, Steve." She gave her high-pitched laugh. "After all, single men are always in demand."

I said I would and hung up.

140

It didn't mean much, but at least, Creeden had been in the city around the time Freda was shot.

I did some more thinking without getting anywhere, then seeing it was now fifteen after midnight I remembered Brenner telling me he would telephone after midnight if he had proof that I was being tailed. So this meant a couple of trained cops were planted outside my building.

I was sure, I told myself, that the second film held the key to all this, but if I was now going to be tailed how was I going to get it, hire a projector and see the film without two cops busting in?

Going to my bank wouldn't be suspicious. I'd take my brief-case with me. I remembered I was going to talk to Ernie about investments. When I left him, I would go down to the vault and get the film. It would be unlikely my tails would know about the vault.

Freddie Dunmore had a photographic studio. He did a lot of art work for me. That too wouldn't be suspicious. He would have a 16 mm. projector. I could talk him into letting me have his projection room for ten minutes.

Thinking about this, I decided it was the only way, but remembering Gordy's killing and now Freda's killing, I would start the day with the gun I had forgotten to give Max.

It was now pushing 01.00. I went into the bedroom and turned down the bed. I took a quick shower, got into my pyjamas and climbed into the strange bed. I realised as I lay there, with the bedside lamp making shadows that after all I did miss my own home. This was something I had to get used to.

If only Jean was by my side, I thought, stretching out in the king-size bed, what a difference all this would make! I wondered about the man she had chosen and I felt a pang of jealousy. Who knows? I told myself, he might get bored with her or she with him and then, maybe I would still stand a chance. As I snapped on the light, I told myself that she was the one woman who meant anything to me. I lay in the darkness and thought of her. Then I remembered something my father told me when I was a kid. My father and I had got along fine together. He was a gentle,

understanding man but he hadn't been wonderfully successful. He had said, "Look, Steve, here's something to think
about. If you ever really want something, never let go.
Hang on and keep hanging on and sooner or later if you
hang on long enough you'll get it." He had smiled and
ruffled my hair. "The trouble with me is I've really never
wanted anything bad enough."

Well, I wanted Jean. Remembering my father's words,
I decided to hang on. With that thought in my mind, I
slipped into sleep.

Dreams are strange things. I kept dreaming that I wasn't
alone. I dreamed a shadowy figure was looking down at
me as I slept. This figure was moving around me: dark,
with no outline: neither man nor woman: just a silent,
sinister figure and I knew, in my dream, this shadowy figure
meant me harm.

I woke with a start. All I could hear was the traffic passing below. I found I was sweating. Then I heard the elevator descend and I looked at the lighted face of the bedside clock. It was 03.40.

I turned over, pulling the bedclothes around my
shoulders.

But I didn't sleep any more that night.

*   *   *

On my way to my office the following morning, I kept
looking in my driving mirror, but the traffic was too heavy
to spot a tail.

Knowing that I was now being watched gave me an
uneasy feeling. I told myself that as soon as I had dealt
with the mail, I would leave Jean to take care of the other
and go over to the bank for the film. With any luck, before
lunchtime I would know who was on the film.

But it wasn't to be. When I walked into the office where
Judy was already at work, she swung around in her typing-
chair.

"Morning, Mr. Manson. Jean called. She's sick."

I came to an abrupt standstill.

"Isn't she coming in?"

142

"Oh, no, Mr. Manson. She's in bed. Something she ate last night."

"Is she bad?"

Judy nodded.

"I think so, but she says she'll be okay tomorrow."

I realised it would now be impossible for me to leave the office until 18.00. If Chandler should call and found both Jean and myself absent there could be trouble.

"I've opened the mail, Mr. Manson, and Miss Shelley from Secretarial Services is already here for dictation," Judy said.

"Fine . . . thanks."

Somehow I got through the morning. It was just as well I hadn't taken a chance and had gone to the bank for Chandler came through soon after 11.00. He thought it was time we began to research Senator Linsky. When I told him Max Berry was already working on it, he was pleased.

Judy got me a sandwich lunch. I told her to give me a direct line and go for her own lunch. That left me alone in the office. She hadn't been gone more than ten minutes when the telephone bell rang. I heard coins dropping into the box, then Brenner came on the line.

"Listen, Manson," he said, "you're being tailed. Don't underestimate these two. They know their job, so watch it."

"Give me a description of them," I said. "I guessed as you didn't call last night I was being tailed, but I haven't spotted them. It'd be a help to know their car and what they look like."

"Dark blue Mustang XP 55001," Brenner told me. "Taylor is tall, thin with dark crewcut, wears sports clothes. O'Hara is short, thickset, red hair, wears dark clothes and a dark blue hat, but it's my bet you won't spot either of them: they're professionals." A pause, then he asked, "Have you looked at that film yet?"

"I can't until tonight."

"You'll have to tell me about it. I'm not taking the chance of being seen with you. You know you're in trouble? I thought you told me that gun was lost."

"I thought so too. It was dumped in a sack of rubbish. Someone must have seen it dumped and collected it."

Brenner grunted.

"Goldstein's working on it. From tomorrow, your apartment phone is going to be tapped."

I stiffened.

"Is this line clean?"

"He can't do anything about that. He's too scared of Chandler to tap anything belonging to him."

"He hasn't a case against me, has he?" I said, feeling my hands turning damp.

"Not yet, but he's got his teeth into you and he'll need shaking off. Take a look at that film and I'll call you this time tomorrow," and he hung up.

I got up and went to the window and looked down on the busy street some eight storeys below. It took me five minutes watching before I spotted Taylor. Without Brenner's description he would have been an anonymous man, but there he was, propping up a fire hydrant while he read a newspaper. I studied him, made sure I would recognise him anywhere, then looked around for his buddy, but O'Hara was not to be seen. He was probably covering the lobby.

Then the telephone bell started up and I was back in the business of producing the magazine.

Around 14.15, I called Jean's apartment.

When she answered, her voice rather far away, I said, "I'm sorry about this, Jean. How do you feel now?"

"I'm recovering. I swear I'll never eat a clam again as long as I live. How are you getting on?"

I told her Judy had everything organised.

"Do you feel like a visit?" I went on. "I could come around after six and bring you something."

"Thank you. It's kind of you but my tummy just couldn't face any visitors."

I felt a pang of disappointment.

"I can imagine." A pause, then I said, "Jean, you remember dumping something in a sack of rubbish?"

"Yes."

"Someone must have followed you and found it."

144

I heard her catch her breath.

"Not now! This line goes through the switchboard. I'll see you tomorrow," and she hung up.

I sat staring at the telephone for a long moment, then replaced the receiver. As I did so there came a tap on my door and Max Berry came in.

From then on until after 17.00, he and I worked on the material he had dug up on Senator Linsky. This was sensational stuff and I told him he had done a fine job. He grinned and said he would get the article written.

Because of the time I had spent with him, I found I had more work left on my desk than I had bargained for. I was still hard at it when Judy looked in to ask if it was all right for her to go home. I looked at my watch and saw it was 18.30.

"Sure. I've talked with Jean. She thinks she'll be in tomorrow. Thanks for all you've done, Judy."

She looked happy.

"Have you nearly finished, Mr. Manson?"

I had still some printer's proofs to go through.

"About an hour." I got up and locked the office door after her, then I went back to my desk and got down to work again.

It was after 19.00 before I had finished. I called Freddie Dunmore at the photographic studio.

"You just caught me, Steve," he said. "I'm in a rush. My wife's throwing a goddamn party and I swore by my back teeth I'd be there on time. What's cooking?"

"I want the use of a 16 mm. projector, Freddie."

"No problem. I'll have it sent over to you tomorrow morning. How's that?"

"I want it tonight."

He groaned.

"Well, okay. I'll leave it with . . ."

"I also want to borrow your projection room tonight," I broke in.

The magazine account with Dunmore was substantial. He was in no position to refuse me.

"God help me! Okay. I'll call Betty . . . she'll kill me."

"Can you leave the key somewhere? I could be late. I'll

run off the film, lock up and return the key. How's that?"

"Can you handle a projector?"

"I guess so."

"Well, okay. For Pete's sake, don't forget to lock up. There's a lot of expensive equipment here I wouldn't want to lose."

"Where do I find the key?"

"On the ledge above the door. It's my spare. God! I'm already twenty minutes late! See you, Steve," and he hung up.

Now I had to lose those two cops. Remembering Brenner's warning, I decided not to rush it. I had most of the night ahead of me.

As I started to the door I paused. Two people had been killed because of the film I was going to collect. I could make a third. I went to the closet and got out the gun that Max Berry hadn't taken away. I loaded it, put on the holster, adjusted my jacket, and turned off the lights. I locked up the office, then carrying my brief-case, I took the elevator to the lobby.

A short, thickset man with red hair, wearing a dark blue hat was examining the indicator board. He didn't look in my direction. He was a pro all right. Even when I paused on the street and glanced back, he was still examining the board.

I got in my car and edged into the traffic. Three minutes later, I spotted the blue Mustang, two cars behind me. It was easy when you knew who and what to look for.

I drove to the Imperial hotel and went into the grill room. Henri, the Captain of waiters, knew me well and welcomed me. I asked for a corner table and sat with my back to the wall, facing the entrance. I ordered the special, then lit a cigarette and toyed with a dry martini while I waited.

After some minutes, Taylor came to the entrance, glanced around, his eyes seeming not to notice me, then he moved back into the lounge.

Henri served me and as trade was quiet, he stood around, saying nice things about the magazine. I was glad to have him. Once again Taylor looked in as if he were expecting a guest, then moved out of sight.

"Henri," I said, when I had finished the meal, "I'm on an assignment this evening for the mag. It's something red hot. A couple of newsmen from the *Sun* are tailing me, hoping to get a lead." I took a ten spot from my hip-pocket and slid it to him. "Is there a way out the back?"

He loved this. His eyes sparkled.

"Through the service door, Mr. Manson, straight ahead, down some steps and the door facing you. It's bolted but not locked. It takes you onto Granby Street."

"Take a look in the lounge. There are two of them: one tall, dark with a crewcut and the other short, red hair. If they look busy, rub the back of your neck."

"Sure, Mr. Manson."

The service door was two yards from me. I pushed back my chair, my heart thumping and watched Henri wander to the entrance. He paused, holding a sheaf of menus as if looking for clients, then he rubbed the back of his neck.

I was out of my chair, through the service door where I nearly cannoned into a waiter, carrying a loaded tray, and down the stairs, eased back the bolt and was in the hot night air.

I had all the luck in the world. An empty cab cruised towards me. I bundled in and told the cabby to take me fast to the Plaza movie house which was within easy range of my bank.

I sat back, breathing heavily. At the end of the narrow street, I looked through the rear window, but the street was deserted. I felt pretty sure I had shaken them off.

Now for the film.

*   *   *

The clerk at the reception desk gave me a smile of welcome as I crossed the lobby.

"Hello there, Mr. Manson. Do you want something from your safe?"

"That's right. Can I go down?"

"Sure. Charlie is down there. He'll take care of you." As I started for the stairs, leading to the vault, he said, "Oh, Mr. Manson, I nearly forgot. I have a telephone message for you."

I started at him.

"For me?"

"Came in half an hour ago." He handed me a slip of paper.

Urgent. Call Western 00798

"If you want to call now, Mr. Manson, there's a booth over to your right."

I went to the booth, put in coins, dialled and waited.

Brenner's voice came on the line. He said: "Who's that?"

"Manson. What is it?"

"This evening Taylor reported to Goldstein that you are being tailed by two of Webber's men. They are smart operators, but Taylor spotted them. Have you any idea why they are tailing you?"

This information so shocked me, I was unable to think. I felt that chill again.

"Manson?"

"I have no idea."

"So you have four pros on your tail. You'd better watch it. Looks like you're in real trouble."

I pulled myself together and forced my mind to work.

"Can you give me a description of them?"

"Sure. I worked with them before they quit to hook up with Webber. Meyer is big, around forty-five, has a broad white scar on his left cheek he got when arresting a junkie. Freeman is big, around fifty and he limps. He had a car smash."

Had these two men followed me to the bank? Why were they following me . . . the film? I felt horribly alone as I stood, sweating in the airless booth.

"You got the film yet?" Brenner asked.

"Not yet."

"Well, watch it," and he hung up.

I leaned against the wall of the booth and thought. I was sure I had shaken off Taylor and O'Hara, but I had no idea if I had shaken off Webber's men. This was no time to take chances. I certainly wasn't going on the streets, carrying that film. But what to do? After a few moments, an idea occurred to me. Leaving the booth, I went down to the vault.

Charlie, fat and elderly and always ready to oblige, got to his feet as I crossed the floor.

"You're late, Mr. Manson."

"Yes. I want to open my safe."

He went with me, turned the first lock with his pass key, then moved away while I opened the second lock with my key. I took out the carton of film.

"Charlie . . . have you a big envelope to take this?" I showed him the carton.

"Sure . . . right here." He produced an envelope. I took the film *cassette* out of its carton and put it in the envelope and sealed it. A bit of flat lead which Charlie probably used as a paperweight caught my eye.

"Want to earn fifty dollars, Charlie?"

His eyes popped open.

"Try me and see, Mr. Manson."

I scribbled Max Berry's address on the envelope.

"Could you deliver this yourself tonight?"

He squinted at the address.

"Why, sure, Mr. Manson. That's not too far from my home, but I won't be off duty until two."

"That's okay. Look, Charlie, this is top secret. It's to do with the magazine. Don't carry it in your hand. Put it inside your jacket. Understand?"

His eyes popped open, but he nodded.

"Let's see you do it."

He unbuttoned his grey uniform jacket and pushed the envelope inside.

"Fine. Keep it like that until you see Mr. Berry." I gave him a fifty dollar bill. Then I picked up the small bar of lead. "Can I have this?"

"Why sure, Mr. Manson."

I put the lead bar in the empty carton to give it weight, then I put the carton in my brief-case.

"Okay, Charlie . . . I'm relying on you."

"You can, Mr. Manson. This envelope . . ." He tapped his chest, "will be with Mr. Berry by half past two."

I went up the stairs and back into the call booth. I called Max. He answered after a delay and he sounded sleepy.

"Max! This is Steve! A messenger from my bank is bringing you a sealed envelope. The contents are dynamite. Two people have been killed because of it and I think Wally got beaten up because of it. Hide it somewhere in your place where it can't be found."

"For God's sake!" Max now sounded very much awake. "What is it?"

"I can't tell you. Don't look at it. The messenger will be arriving around two-thirty. Stay with it until I telephone you tomorrow from the office."

"Okay Steve."

Before leaving the booth, I eased the gun in its holster and satisfied myself it would come out fast, then holding the brief-case firmly under my arm, I walked out into the night.

Moving fast down the street, I looked anxiously for a cab, but this time I had no luck.

More than anytime before, I felt someone breathing down my neck. I kept looking over my shoulder. At this time of the night the down town section of the city was almost deserted.

Then it happened.

I didn't even see them.

I felt the brief-case jerk away from under my arm and I received a stunning, chopping blow at the back of my neck.

I was still on my hands and knees, trying to clear my head when I heard a car start up and drive away.

nine

As THE cab drove me to the Imperial hotel, I nursed my aching neck with both hands and reviewed the situation.

When Webber's men realised I had sold them a dummy —and it wouldn't take long—they would come after me. I realised that I was out of their class, so I needed police protection. I had it without asking for it! As soon as Taylor and O'Hara picked me up they would stay with me, and I had no intention now of losing them. With them watching me, Webber's men wouldn't risk moving in on me.

Still unsteady on my legs, I paid off the cabby and walked to where I had left my car. I saw the blue Mustang was parked five bays from mine. Taylor was sitting at the wheel. There was no sign of O'Hara.

I got in my car and drove to my apartment. From time to time I checked my driving mirror. The Mustang was following. I drove into the underground garage, then took the elevator to my apartment.

As the cage arrived at my floor, I took out the gun and held it down by my side. I couldn't be sure Webber's men had found out they had no film and had already arrived.

I stepped from the cage onto the corridor, looked to right and left, saw nothing to alarm me, stepped across to my front door, unlocked it, moved into the lobby, shut the door and switched on the light. I then pushed open the living-room door, stood back as I reached for the light switch and snapped it up. No one there. I paused to lock the front door and shoot the bolt, then moving carefully, I explored the apartment. They hadn't arrived.

For the moment I was safe. Short of battering down the door, no one could get in.

I put the gun on the table crossed over to the liquor cabinet. I poured myself a stiff shot of whisky and dropped into a lounging chair.

I thought about what had happened. The question that baffled me was why Webber was involved. Until Brenner had alerted me, I had no reason to suspect that Webber's men were shadowing me. How long had they been doing this? My mind shifted to Creeden. He had enough money to hire Webber. If his wife was on the film, then he would need help and Webber would be the man to hire.

I finished my drink, set down the glass and got to my feet.

I was sure the key to all this was on the film that Max had, but did he have it? Had Webber guessed what I had done and had sent his men after Charlie?

I dialled Max's number.

The time now was 03.15.

There was a long delay, then Max mumbled, "Who the hell is this?"

"Steve. Did you get it? Answer yes or no . . . nothing else."

"For the sake of Judas! Yes!"

I hung up.

I went into the lonely bedroom stripped off my clothes and flopped on the bed. My neck was aching, my body limp and exhausted. I lay like that, my mind churning, until finally sleep came.

The following morning, with the Mustang following me, I drove to my office. I felt secure with these two cops tailing me. They would give Webber's men no room to manoeuvre.

Judy greeted me with a smile.

"Jean says she'll be in after lunch, Mr. Manson. She still sounds pretty bad. Miss Shelley is here and waiting."

"Thanks, Judy."

I dealt with the mail, then when Miss Shelley, a dumpy, serious-looking girl who dwelt behind enormous glasses, had gone into Jean's office to type, I called Freddie Dunmore.

"Freddie . . . I didn't make it last night. I want that projector. Will you send it over?"

"Sure Steve."

"Wrap it. I don't want anyone here to know it's a projector."

A pause, then he said, "James Bond Stuff, huh?"

"That's the idea. Make a parcel of it and get it over here fast."

"Will and can do," and he hung up.

I then called Max Berry.

"Bring that envelope over right away, Max. Put it under your jacket. As I told you, it's dynamite."

"Okay, Steve. I'm on my way."

There was nothing else I could do now but to hope. Although I hadn't the time to spare, I told Judy to call Jean for me.

While I was wrestling with a heap of mail, the call came through.

"Jean! How do you feel?"

"I'm all right. I told Judy to tell you I'll be in after lunch. I'm still a bit queazy, but I'll survive."

"Don't come in unless you're really fit."

"I'm coming in."

I couldn't resist it.

"I've missed you."

"Thank you. I'll be in," and the line went dead.

My old man had told me to hang on. I wasn't getting any encouragement, but I loved her, I wanted her, I needed her, so I was going to hang on.

I settled down to read Rafferty's film column that had come in the mail. I was only half concentrating. Suddenly, I got up, went to the window and looked down on the street. This time it was O'Hara who was propping up the fire hydrant. The sight of him was reassuring. As long as he was there I couldn't imagine Webber's men visiting me. Taylor was probably covering the lobby.

The intercom buzzed.

"There's a parcel for you, Mr. Manson," Judy told me. "Shall I bring it in."

"Thanks."

It was the projector, carefully wrapped. A note from Freddie saying he enclosed the instruction book and if I was in trouble to call him.

I put the projector in a closet and finished the Rafferty article. I okayed it and tossed it in my out-tray. As I was starting to read a short story submitted by one of my agents, Max Berry came in.

"Here it is," he said, putting the envelope on my desk. "What's the big excitement about, Steve? You got me out of bed twice last night. What's all this about dynamite?"

"No comment, Max, for the moment," I said. "Thanks for bringing it. How's the Linsky article building?"

He gaped at me.

"For Pete's sake, is that all you're going to say?"

"That's all. How's the Linsky article building?"

"I'll have it finished tomorrow." He eyed the envelope, looked questioningly at me, then said, "Well, if that's all, I'll get back to it."

"Do that and thanks again."

Looking mystified, he left me.

I stared at the envelope, then looked at my desk clock. The time was close to mid day. In another quarter of an hour, Judy would be going to lunch and I would have the office to myself. I put the envelope in my desk drawer, then tried to settle to reading the short story but concentration was impossible. I was sweating and my heart was thumping. In a few minutes now I could know the truth unless Freda had sold me a pup. There was always that chance, but thinking back, seeing her serious eyes, hearing her say, 'Boy scout's honor' I felt sure this was the film now in my desk drawer that had caused her and Gordy's death.

The minutes dragged by. I wanted to get up and tell Judy to go, but I restrained myself.

It wasn't until 12.20 that she looked in.

"All right for me to go to lunch, Mr. Manson?"

"Sure."

She nodded brightly and I heard her go off to the rest

room. At 12.30 I heard her leave. I went to the outer door and locked it. I had only an hour before she returned. Then hurrying back to my office I got out the projector and set it on my desk. Opposite was a blank white wall. My hands were unsteady as I ripped open the envelope and took out the *cassette*. It was a self-loading job, but even at that I spent a few minutes before I got it loaded. I pulled out the plug of my electric desk clock and connected up the projector. Then I lowered the sun blinds and pulled the curtains.

As I returned to my desk, the telephone bell rang.

The sound made my heart skip a beat. For a long moment, I hesitated, then I lifted the receiver.

"Mr. Manson? Mr. Chandler on the line."

Sweat dripped off my chin.

"Steve? Come over and have lunch with me. I've got some real poison that will fix Linsky. I want to discuss it with you."

I sat staring at the projector.

"You there, Steve? Come right over. We'll have a working lunch here."

Trying to steady my voice, I said, "I can't make it, Mr. Chandler. Jean's away sick and Judy's just gone to lunch."

"Well, lock up! The office won't run away. Come on over!" and he hung up.

That was something I was not going to do. I switched on the projector, moving the focusing ring as a picture appeared on the white wall. I found myself looking down one of the aisles, packed either side with groceries, of the Welcome store.

It was an excellent picture. I could even read the labels on some of the cans. There were no customers, which puzzled me. After a few moments the scanner shifted and I caught a glimpse of a suspended clock. The time showed 09.03. The store had just opened. Now the picture showed where you got hard liquor. Then from around a corner, pushing a market cart, came a woman. As she walked, she was looking over her shoulder as if to make sure no one was watching her. She paused by the whisky section, then looked fully into the lens of the hidden scanner.

My heart skipped a beat and I heard myself gasp.

The woman was Jean!

My hand turned into fists and my nails dug into my palms.

She was looking down the aisle, her expression expectant. Seldom do you see that expression but I had seen it before and I recognised it. It was the look of a lover, waiting for a lover.

Then a man moved into the picture: tall, heavily built, wearing a black hat and a city suit. There was something horribly familiar about his broad back. He caught Jean in his arms and she flung her arms around his neck. They kissed the way only starved lovers kiss.

So brief, and yet to me it was like a knife thrust in my heart. Then he moved back, giving her a warning sign, and I saw his face.

It was Henry Chandler!

*　　*　　*

The telephone bell rang.

With a shaking hand I turned off the projector, then lifted the receiver.

"Mr. Manson?" I recognised Chandler's secretary's sharp voice. "Mr. Chandler is waiting."

"Tell him I am held up."

"He won't like that, Mr. Manson."

"I'm sorry," and I replaced the receiver. I ran the film back into the *cassette*, took it off the projector, removed the plug, then moving like an automaton, I put the projector into my closet, the *cassette* in my pocket and pulled up the blinds. As I did so, the telephone bell rang again.

It was Chandler and there was an angry rasp in his voice.

"What's going on? I'm waiting. You're holding up my lunch!"

I found myself hating him. The thought of eating with him, even looking at him, knowing Jean loved him, revolted me.

"I have a client with me, Mr. Chandler," I said wooden-ly. "I can't get away."

"Who is it?" he barked.

"Mr. Coulston, the advertising executive for Hartmans."

Hartmans was one of our most important advertisers.

A pause, then Chandler said irritably, "Well, all right. Why didn't you say so? Okay, I'll send the stuff about Linsky over right away. I'm booked solid this afternoon. You read it and come to my place for dinner. We'll discuss it, huh?"

"I'll read it and telephone you, Mr. Chandler. I have a long-standing date for tonight," and not giving a damn, I hung up.

I stared at the blank white wall which only a few minutes ago had showen me Jean and Chandler embracing.

She and he! That they were lovers was obvious. I had only to remember the expression of love and longing on Jean's face to know that was a fact. How Gordy must have rubbed his hands when he had run off the film.

Henry Chandler, the leading citizen, the leading Quaker who had built the city's church! Chandler, who owned the magazine who threw stones at people! Chandler who had amassed two hundred million dollars and was on first name terms with the President caught on film in a self-service store (of all places) kissing a girl who had been his fourth secretary! No wonder Gordy had told Freda the film was worth a million dollars. If it became public property, Chandler was finished!

Sitting there, still shaking, I remembered his words when I accepted his offer to edit *The Voice of the People.* Those words now burned into my brain:

You will be attacking the corrupt and the dishonest. Remember you will be a goldfish in a bowl. Be careful: don't give anyone a chance to hit back at you. Take me: I'm a Quaker. I believe in God. My private life can't be criticised. No finger can point to me and no one must be able to point a finger at you.

You hypocrite! I thought. You bloody, bloody hypo-crite! You set yourself up as the second God to be a

157

scourge of the corrupt and the dishonest and you're even worse than any of them because, behind your sanctimonious facade, you are a liar, an adulterer and a cheat!

I was shaking with rage and my body was cold. I wanted to ruin him. I wanted to expose him for what he was. I could do it! I could get Dunmore to blow up one of the frames and I could put the blow-up on the cover of *The Voice of the People*. I wouldn't even have to write a commentary. That picture alone would bring him and his empire crashing down!

My searing thoughts were disturbed by the sound of knocking. I controlled my rage, looked at my watch and saw it was 13.02. I walked unsteadily into the outer office and unlocked the door.

Judy came in.

"Did you have lunch, Mr. Manson?" she asked as she put her handbag on the desk. "I'll get you a sandwich if you like."

The thought of food revolted me.

"It's okay. I'm busy," and I went back to my office and shut the door.

I sat at my desk. Judy with her freshness and youth had broken the thread of my rage. I began to think rationally. If it hadn't been Jean, who I loved, but for the sake of argument, it had been Judy on that film, would I have reacted the way I had been reacting? I knew at once that I wouldn't have. It was because this rich, Quaker hypocrite had taken Jean from me that I had been in this revengeful rage. If it had been any other woman except Jean I would have been surprised, shrugged my shoulders and have destroyed the film.

I picked up my paper-knife and began to dig holes in my blotter.

A man and a woman meet, I thought. Some kind of chemistry takes place and suddenly they are in love. Are either of them to blame? It had taken months for me suddenly to realise Jean was the woman I wanted: my chemistry had been diluted by Linda. Chandler had been ahead of me. When this chemistry explosion happens and when you are in a vulnerable position of a goldfish in a

Quaker bowl, what are you to do? It would depend, I told myself, how big the explosion had been. If it was merely a sudden sex urge, then it should be resisted, but if it was real love . . . ?

Chandler couldn't ask for a divorce. Lois was the kind of woman who would fight tooth and nail to hold onto what she had. He would have to make the reason known and this would bring him down. So he was faced with meeting Jean in sneaky places like the Welcome store and God knows what other places for a hurried kiss.

So to keep his sanctimonious reputation, two worthless people had been murdered. Who had killed them? Certainly not Chandler. When you had unlimited money as Chandler had there was no problem to hire a professional gunman. Borg did all Chandler's dirty work. He could easily hire some killer to walk into Gordy's house and shoot him.

I paused in my thinking and realised I was letting my imagination run away with me.

Gordy and Freda had been shot with my gun. A professional killer would have used his own gun! So it was unlikely that those two had been killed by a hired gunman.

Then who?

I pressed my hands against my hot face.

Why should I care? I asked myself. Why should I care if a blackmailer and a drunken hustler died?

But I did care that Jean was Chandler's mistress. The shock was still with me. She had said she was coming to the office this afternoon. I felt in no state to face her. If she came, I knew I couldn't stay in the office. I had to have time to adjust.

I asked Judy for an outside line, then called Jean's number. She answered almost at once.

"This is Steve," I said. "Please don't come in today, Jean."

"But I'm just on my way." Her voice sounded low and unsteady.

"Please stay at home. There is nothing for you to do. Come in tomorrow."

A long pause, then she said, "Well, all right."

I put down the receiver as Judy came in with a sealed envelope from Chandler.

"Jean won't be in until tomorrow," I told her.

"I'm not surprised. I once had clam poisoning and it nearly killed me."

When she had left me, I tossed the envelope into my in-tray. *The Voice of the People* was now such a symbol of hypocrisy to me I had no further interest in it.

I pulled my I.B.M. towards me and wrote the following letter:

Henry Chandler,
I can no longer work for you. Accept this as my resig-
nation from today. There is enough material for the next
issue. The editorial staff of your newspaper will be able to
bring out the magazine.
As you once said to me: goldfish have no hiding place.
Goldfish in a Quaker bowl have none at all.
                                      Steve Manson.

I put the note in an envelope, marked it 'Private and Personal', sealed it, then asked Judy to have it sent over to the Chandler building by special delivery.

"I'm not taking any telephone calls nor seeing any visitors, Judy," I said. "I don't want to be disturbed. Say I am out and won't be back until tomorrow."

Her eyes popped open wide.

"Well, okay, Mr. Manson."

"That includes Mr. Chandler. If he calls, I'm still out."

I went back to my office and locked the door.

I spent the next two hours clearing my desk and putting all the material, the notes, the sketched ideas for the next issue of the magazine together.

I heard Judy answering the telephone from time to time. I wondered what would happen to her. My own future didn't worry me. I had money in the bank, I was free of Linda and I could return to Los Angeles where I could become a freelance.

Finally, around 18.00, I had completed the clearing up. Everything was in order. One of the bright boys on the

California Times could pick up where I had left off, but that didn't mean *The Voice of the People* would survive. I hoped it wouldn't.

Carrying my bulging brief-case, I went into the outer office.

Poor Judy looked bothered.

"Oh, Mr. Manson, Mr. Chandler has twice called asking for you."

"That's all right, Judy. Don't worry about a thing. You get off home." I smiled at her. "Will you lock up? I'm through for the day."

The telephone bell rang. Judy picked up the receiver as I opened the outer door.

"Mr. Manson!" she hissed. "It's Mr. Chandler."

"I'm still out," I said and crossing the corridor, I rode the elevator down for the last time and with no regrets.

*　　*　　*

As I drove towards my apartment, I began to make plans. There was a midnight plane to Los Angeles. I would pack and get out. Once back on my old home ground I was sure I would be able to adjust myself. The loose ends like the apartment lease, my personal things could be tied up later, but this city was now suffocating me. I had to have four or five days away from it.

Looking in my driving mirror, I spotted the blue Mustang following me. I didn't give a damn. I wondered how the cops would react when they followed me to the airport and watched me board a plane for L.A. They couldn't stop me. They wouldn't know I wasn't on an assignment for the magazine.

I left the Merc in the parking bay and went up to my apartment, imagining Taylor and O'Hara settling down to a long and dreary wait.

I unlocked my front door and walked into the lobby. The door leading to the living-room was half open and I saw the lights were on. I was still carrying Max's gun. Dropping my brief-case, I got the gun into my hand, then kicked the door wide open and stood in the doorway.

I was expecting to be faced my Webber's men, but instead, facing me, looking a ghost of herself, was Jean.

Slowly, I lowered the gun.

As I stared at her, the thought came into my mind—the same thought that had come into my mind when I put the bottle of Chanel No. 5 in front of Linda—was this the woman I was in love with?

I continued to look at her and as I looked the fragile light of love flickered and went out. I was facing a stranger: white faced, gaunt, hard and perhaps even dangerous.

My eyes moved from her and I looked around the room. It had been wrecked. Every possible hiding place had been explored with frantic frenzy. Even the cushions in the chairs and the settee had been ripped open. The stuffing, like little white islands, lay on the floor. Every drawer had been emptied: its contents thrown anyhow.

I tossed my gun on the ripped settee and walked into the bedroom. That too was wrecked. Even the mattress had been slit open. My clothes lay on the floor. Every drawer had been emptied and its contents spilled everywhere.

I returned to the living-room. She still stood motionless, pressed against the wall, her eyes like two red hot embers.

"Joe Borg will love this," I said quietly. "He'll probably sue you."

"Where is it?" she said, her voice husky.

I regarded her, then I knew and I felt a cold chill run over me.

"Is that how you looked when you shot Gordy?" I asked. "Did you say that to him . . . where is it? Is that how you looked when you shot that stupid, drunken hooker?"

She lifted her right hand and I saw she had a gun.

"Tell me or I'll kill you! Where is it?"

I looked at the gun . . . my gun. That story about putting the gun in a sack of rubbish! She had kept it and had killed again with it! Looking at her, I was sure she was now mentally unbalanced and yet I had no fear of her. I was just sick that I had lost her, that my stupid dreams that she would get bored with this other man and then she and I could come together were finished.

I took the film *cassette* from my pocket and held it out to her.

"Here it is, Jean," I said. "Why didn't you confide in me?"

She remained motionless, the gun pointing at me, then slowly her wild eyes moved from me to the *cassette*. She caught her breath in a retching sob.

"Really?"

"Freda Hawes sold it to me for fifteen hundred dollars," I said. "Here it is, Jean . . . take it."

The gun dropped from her hand. She came forward and snatched the *cassette* and held it against her face, then she fell on her knees. She began to moan softly like a small animal in agony.

I picked up the gun and tossed it by Max's gun on the settee. My legs felt unsteady and my head was beginning to ache. I was so very sick of all this. I sat on the arm of a ruined armchair and watched her, cradling the *cassette* and muttering to herself. This, I thought, must be a proof of love and I wished Chandler was here to see her.

Minutes ticked away. I just sat there, waiting.

Finally she stopped moaning and muttering.

"I'll get you a drink," I said and went to the liquor cabinet and poured a stiff brandy.

She was now on her feet, clutching the *cassette,* her eyes less wild.

"I don't want it!"

"Drink it!"

The glass chattered against her teeth, but she drank the brandy. She shuddered as she set down the glass.

"This really is the film?" she asked huskily.

"That's it. You and Chandler. I'm leaving the city. If you'll go now, I'll be able to get on with my packing."

She dropped onto one of the slashed cushions.

"I love him. He is the perfect man. Ever since I began to work for him, I loved him. I would do anything for him. I have done everything for him." She stared at me. "You wouldn't know what real love means. So few people do: to make sacrifices, to do anything for the person you love." She pressed her hands against her face. "The moment I met him I fell in love with him: It took longer for him to love me. He is such a fine, splendid man. We knew our love for each other had to be kept secret and yet we yearned for each other. It became too dangerous for me to work with him. There were so many prying eyes and we knew if we worked together we would give ourselves away. So he sent me to work for you. Yet we had to meet." She closed her eyes. "Those awful, furtive places: a movie house when I had to search for him in the dark, taxi rides that were dangerous, dreadful little bars and then the Welcome store." Her voice faltered. "We thought we were so clever going to the Welcome store early, but we didn't know about the camera." She lifted her shoulders helplessly. "There was nothing more. Only the touch of his lips, the feel of his hands ... that was all."

Listening to all this sickened me.

"Please stop," I said. "You have the film. Please go away. I have packing to do."

"I want to confess." Her eyes became red embers again. "I have so much to confess. Gordy came to me. He hadn't the guts to go to Henry. He told me about the film. His price was a million dollars. Sneering at me, he said Henry and I were in good company, and he mentioned these other women's names I told you Wally had given me. Wally knew nothing about the Welcome store. I lied when I told you he had been researching. How else could I gain your confidence? I needed as much information as I could get. The attack on Wally was nothing to do with Gordy. It was mugging. I realised I had to have help so I went to Webber. Without Henry, Webber is nothing and he knows it. He is the only one who knows Henry and I love each other. He knew this woman Hawes was close to Gordy. He went to her apartment when she was out and found blow-ups which he destroyed as he destroyed Gordy's file so you shouldn't have it. In the file was Gordy's past record. He had served ten years for blackmail. I was scared if you knew this you might scare Gordy into talking about Henry and me.", She rubbed her hand across her forehead. "With the blow-ups destroyed, I had to get the film. I needed a gun. I planned to frighten Gordy into giving me the film.

I knew you had a gun and I followed you home, watched you leave, found the front door unlocked and got the gun. I drove to Gordy's house. I threatened him and he laughed at me so I shot him." She paused to look around the wrecked room, her face a wooden mask. "It was a crazy thing to have done because I hadn't the film. I realised the police might be able to prove I had killed him and that would involve Henry." She looked directly at me. "So I decided to make you responsible for Gordy's death. You mean nothing to me. You never have. I know you think you are in love with me." Her face twitched in a grimace of disgust. "To me that is an obscene joke. Compare yourself with Henry and you will see why. It seemed easy. I had your gun. Webber's men never let you out of their sight. They got the reel of tape which would incriminate you. They also got the film when you found it, showing your wife stealing. You can't imagine how I suffered when I discovered there had to be a second film. That police lieutenant is dangerous. I decided to kill you." She paused and shuddered, looking away from me. "Please, try to understand that all this was driving me out of my mind. I have duplicate keys to all Borg's apartments. I came here the other night with the tape, the film and the gun. You were asleep. I planned to shoot you, leaving the tape, the film and the gun by your side. I was sure the police would think you had killed yourself. I stood over you, the gun at your head, but I couldn't pull the trigger. I stayed by you for a long time, but something stopped me, so in despair, I went away and I destroyed the tape and the film. Webber told me you had met this Hawes woman. I went to her place and met her as she was returning home. She had an overnight-bag and I felt sure she had the film in it. I shot her." Her face twisted as if she had suffered a pang of pain. "God forgive me! She was so arrogant. She spat at me . . . so I shot her. There was no film. So I came here . . . my last hope. I hunted and hunted and searched and searched. Now I have it." Her face went to pieces and she began to sob. "The joke against me is that Henry knows nothing . . . nothing . . . nothing about all this. He has no idea, and and he never will, what I have done for him .. . .

165

what I have done to protect him. He is living in that lovely house with that stupid, snob, horrible bitch and he imagines I am happy because he sneaks away twice a week to give me a kiss and to touch my hands."

I got to my feet and wandered around the wrecked room. Listening to her sobbing made no impact on me. I just wanted to get away.

"This is something you will have to live with, Jean," I said. "How you work it out, is your affair. I'm sorry you think my love for you is an obscene joke. Will you please go now?"

She stiffened and choked back her sobs.

"Yes, of course." She got unsteadily to her feet. "You could never understand." She clutched the *cassette* in her hand. "You don't know what love means."

I wanted to be rid of her. Maybe she was right. Maybe I didn't know what love meant, but if it meant the death of two people, no matter how worthless, I didn't want to know.

I walked to the door and opened it.

"Goodbye, Jean."

She moved forward, then paused, looking at me.

"Will you do something for me?"

"If I can."

She held out the *cassette*.

"Will you destroy it, please?"

"That's your business, Jean."

"Please . . . do it for me."

"All right." I took the *cassette* and dropped it into my pocket. She moved slowly by me and out into the corridor. She turned and looked at me.

"Thank you. Goodbye, Steve."

I regarded her. How odd, I thought, that this woman had at one time seemed to me the only woman for me. I looked at her haggard, white face and the misery in her eyes and I was looking at a stranger.

"Goodbye."

I was glad to shut the door and see the last of her. After wandering around the wrecked room for some minutes, I went to the telephone and called Borg. When he came on the line, I said, "I have had burglars in here, Joe. The place is completely wrecked. I'm leaving for Los Angeles in an hour. Will you handle it?"

"Have you called the police?"

"I haven't the time to tangle with the police. You do that."

"Hell! I'll get Jean to handle it."

"I would handle it myself if I were you," I said and hung up.

I packed two suitcases, then I picked up the gun that had shot Gordy and Freda and went down to the basement I dropped the gun in the rubbish tip which was constantly smothered with refuse and I dropped the *cassette* into the furnace. I returned to the apartment, picked up my bags and rode down in the elevator to my car.

I had more than two hours before my plane to Los Angeles took off. I drove slowly to the airport, aware the blue Mustang was following me. Leaving my car at the airport garage, I checked my bags in, then went into the bar. I didn't feel like eating. I sat in a corner, nursing a whisky on the rocks and thought about Jean. I thought about what she had told me and I longed to be in the aircraft, flying away from this city.

Eventually, after what seemed an eternity, my flight number was called and I walked across the tarmac to the waiting plane. I embarked, sat, smoked and tried to consider my future. My thoughts kept being interrupted by the picture of Chandler and Jean standing in the aisle of the Welcome store. That picture, I knew, was going to haunt me for a long time.

On arrival, I collected my bags and started across the lobby in search of a cab.

"Mr. Manson?"

I looked around at a tall, lean man who was smiling at me.

"I'm Terry Rogers of the *Hollywood Reporter.*" His smile broadened into a grin. "The grapevine told me you were on the plane. Mr. Manson, is it correct that you have resigned as editor of *The Voice of the People?*"

"That is correct."

"Was there a difference of opinion between you and Mr. Chandler?"

"No. I decided the editorial chair isn't for me." I began to move away from him.

"Sorry about your secretary."

I paused and eyed him.

"My secretary?"

"Miss Jean Kersey. She was your secretary, wasn't she?"

"Yes. What about her?"

"Came over the tape about ten minutes ago. She walked under a truck."

I felt no reaction. It had to end that way.

"Did she?"

"When he heard, Mr. Chandler said it was a very sad loss for the magazine. Have you any comment, Mr. Manson?"

"All of us have to die some time—even goldfish," I said and left him, staring after me.

THE END

〉〉〉 If you've enjoyed this book and would like to discover more great vintage crime and thriller titles, as well as the most exciting crime and thriller authors writing today, visit: 〉〉〉

The Murder Room
Where Criminal Minds Meet

themurderroom.com

www.ingramcontent.com/pod-product-compliance
Ingram Content Group UK Ltd.
Pitfield, Milton Keynes, MK11 3LW, UK
UKHW022308280225
455674UK00004B/226